# SURVIVING ME

## Reginald Raab

PublishAmerica
Baltimore

*Isabelle,*
*you are a great*
*student. I am*
*so glad you*
*are in*
*my class.*

*I had so much*
*fun writing*
*the story*

*I hope you*
*enjoy it.*

*Reginald Raab*

Hardcover 978-1-4512-6311-4
Softcover 978-1-4512-6312-1
PUBLISHED BY PUBLISHAMERICA, LLLP
www.publishamerica.com
Baltimore

Printed in the United States of America

# Dedication

This book is dedicated to my mother who gave me a life rich with experiences, my wife who had courage when she needed it most, and to Ben, Halle, and Nancy who have inspired my in a countless number of ways. I also dedicate this book to all reluctant readers who need a book that makes them laugh but may surprise and teach them a lesson along the way.

# Acknowledgment

I want to thank the many friends and family who took the time to read my work and give constructive criticism, the staff at Pine Street Elementary especially Janet Johnson, and Travis Jonker for their feedback, and the students of my language arts classes who I read the story to in order to gauge its appeal. I set out to have fun and adventure in the open spaces of imagination. What I found was a whole new world and a cup of encouragement for my students. By honing my own skills I have expanded the abilities of my students exponentially.

# Labor Day Break Bites Back

I *thought* this was going to be the best year of my life. I was about to start high school (the big leagues) and everything seemed to be going great. I *thought* that small towns were the safest place under the sun. Now I'm just trying to survive…

I live in Middleville, Michigan. I know what you're thinking *Middleville is that a real town?* The answer is yes! Go ahead and Google it. It really does exist. It got its name because it's half way between the two largest cities in the area, Grand Rapids and Kalamazoo—and maybe Halfwayville didn't sound as good.

It's not the most exciting place in the world. Nothing really ever happens. At least that's what I *use* to think. The only famous guy to live here was Paul Frenchmen (the comedian), who's actually Polish. He goes buy the name French Fry. You might have seen him on HBO or the Comedy Channel. I saw him one night at my friend Marc's house (I had to go there because we don't have cable. My mom has phobias about everything and says it will rot your brain). Marc is a total comedy nut and probably the funniest guy I know. Well, we were watching this French Fry guy. His whole act is about how there is nothing to do in a small town. People in New York and Los Angeles love his act. They think he's making it all up. The fact of it is that it's *all true*. One of his most famous lines is: "The only thing buzzing in a small town are the mosquitoes in the summer and the snow mobiles in the winter." I don't think that is all that funny but the mosquitoes *can* be really bad in the summer.

So anyway I live in Middleville. My best friends all live in the neighborhood with me. There's Marc who I told you a little about. There's Wyoming who's big enough to have a state named after him. There's Chondra or "C" as we call her a lot of the time. She's the only girl friend I have. She's not my girlfriend she's like one of the guys. And then there's Buckley—who just moved into our neighborhood. He's super smart but not very physical. He could get beat up by his own shadow on a windy day.

I guess I'm getting a little ahead of myself. I should take you back to the day that things started to happen to me. I was sitting on the bus sweaty and stinky. The bus was not helping the situation—it was like a mobile locker-room crossing the equator. I sat there disgusted by the bureaucracy that kept the windows closed. I mean the bus is lined with windows but we have to keep them closed for "our own safety." Apparently they didn't take the time to discover the windows were too small for anyone to fit through. If they had to endure this smell they would understand the real life threatening situation.

In the back row of the bus Alabama Jackson; a senior who had moved in from Mississippi, was picking on my friend Marc. Alabama was having *his* version of fun, punching Marc in the shoulder. With each punch he would look up to the front of the bus to see if the driver was looking back. If she did, he would give her his best Eddie Haskell smile and pretend to be as innocent as an angel. If you looked at Alabama when he did this you would swear he had a hallo over his head.

Marc just grimaced after each agonizing punch. He knew the persnickety driver wouldn't do anything. She was always mumbling things like, "stupid kids…" and "their parents must be idiots too…"

My eyes met the hungry eyes of Alabama. I quickly turned my head back toward the front. My thoughts automatically turned back to their normal pattern—Girls, pain, girls, school, girls, lunch, and girls—.

The bus moaned to a stop. I got up from my sweaty seat.

"You're next Thompson," Alabama grinned. The remains of his last few victims were stuck between his teeth.

*Great* I thought.

"Marc stuck his head up from behind the seat. "Meet me for a game in the yard later—ow!"

Alabama smiled at the bus driver.

I crossed my yard dodging the sprinklers, stepped in the house, and flipped off my football cleats on the slate entryway. Clumps of sod flew through the air as they hit the back wall of the coat closet adding texture to the Jackson Polick earth-tone of scuff marks.

"Is that you Ben?" my mom asked from down the hall.

"Yeah mom."

"How was practice?"

I didn't feel like a long conversation, and mom was famous for those so I decided not to respond. I headed down stairs to take off the football gear. Two-a-day practice for the week had taken its' toll but at least I had the long Labor Day weekend before school started on Tuesday.

Starting high school is a big deal and it was on my mind and the minds of all my friends. That—well and of course—girls.

I changed clothes and headed up to get a small snack: two or three sandwiches, some juice, milk, some chips, and cookies. For a teenage boy this *is* a small snack. My mom says somewhere along the line boys get the appetite of Shaggy Rogers. You know—the guy from Scooby Doo who was always hungry.

I pushed aside my dad's cold cup of coffee and started chowing. The morning paper was left on the table. The headline read: **War on Terror: Oil Supply Threatened.** I flipped the page thinking *oil is a weird thing to go to war over*. The next article that caught my eye said: **First writer to make one billion dollars.**

*Wow,* I thought.

I put on my shoes—not bothering to tie them, and started out the door with the last of my sandwich in my mouth. "See you later mom. Goin down by the river," I announced in a sandwich muffle.

I heard her ask "Where you goin?" as I was closing the door.

When I arrived it was pretty churned up from the recent rain. There was a pile of scrap wood and a heavy rope on the bank. I assumed Marc left it there. We talked about making some upgrades to our favorite spot. I gazed up at the tattered rope that hung from an old Swiss cheese limb on the big oak. "I might as well hang this up and surprise everyone," I mumbled to myself. "But first a quick dip!" I announced with a grin.

I tossed off everything but my blue jean cutoffs, unhooked the bungee cord on our tire swing, and took a full speed run from the bank. The tire raced across the river and up toward the trees on the other side. I could feel my stomach lurch as it reached the apex. I swung back over the river and let loose with a primeval cry hitting the cool muddy water with a splash.

As I made my way to the shore I felt a sharp pain in my rear. I screamed, "Yeow!"

I was caught on something heavy and it was pulling me down, down, down. I fought my way trying to climb up the mud soaked embankment. There were some exposed tree roots and I reached for them but they had a weak hold and ripped out sending me falling back into the murky clutches of the river.

The current was dragging me down stream and whatever had a hold of me had not let go. I reached into the water behind me to try and free myself. My hand vanished from existence as it pierced the shroud of the muddy water.

The pain was increasing as I felt behind me. Whatever it was felt razor sharp and was cutting in deep.

I groped around with both hands behind my back. My hands came in contact with something hard and slimy. I felt bumpy edges. Then something razor sharp like a claw scratched my hand. I pulled my hand out of the water and blood started to run down my pinky finger as soon it came out.

I came across a downed limb and pulled myself to shore. Something was banging against my legs with each step. I looked over my shoulder and my eyes popped out of my head. I screamed, "aaaaaaaaaaaaaah!" and took off running. I instinctively grabbed the tattered rope which went up to the old tree fort. Adrenaline was racing through my body. Maybe it was the added weight I was pulling up, or the fact that I was climbing so fast, but the last thing I remember was the sound of the rope snapping...

# I'll have some turtle soup and make it snappy

I drifted back into consciousness laying on the couch.

"No. The hospital will take care of it with your insurance company," a voice said.

I rolled my head to the side to see what was going on.

"Thanks again. And have a good night." My dad began to close the door from the cool air sneaking in.

A portly ambulance driver turned back toward my parents. "He'll be fine Mrs. Thompson. You just get yourself some rest."

\*\*\*

I awoke to the smell of something unusual simmering in the kitchen. It wasn't pancakes and syrup or the smoky aroma of sliced bacon. That was my favorite morning smell. This scent reminded me a little of chicken but it was slightly more wild.

I sat up and tried to figure out why I had slept on the couch. I tossed the blanket off me and screamed, "aaaaaaaaaaaaaaaah. Why am I wearing a diaper?"

My mom entered the room "How's my boy?" She sat next to me and smothered me with affection.

"Mom! Why am I wearing a diaper?" I wiggled out of her embrace for some space.

"We were so worried about you when your friends came and told us they found you knocked out by the river. The ambulance drivers bandaged you up and put that diaper over the top to hold the bandages on. I was so worried about you honey." She was kissing me on the cheek. Her long red hair draped my shoulders.

I tried to pull away. "I know you were worried—don't you remember that essay I wrote in fourth grade. ""What my mom is good at." My mom is good at making grill cheese sandwiches and worrying that something bad will happen to me.""

She had a smile forming in the corner of her mouth from this memory but forced herself back into a more serious discussion. "Your father called the Snyders, Finkbeiners, Johnsons, and the Ruppers looking for you. Marc said you didn't show up for the touch football he invited you to. We didn't know what to think. I was about the call the police, but your father said we should look around the neighborhood ourselves first. You know your father, he kept saying everything will be fine—we were about to give up and dial 911—when your sister spotted you. We were *so* worried." She gave me another hug.

"Are you hungry? Your dad made waffles" Mom got up and made her way out of the room.

"Sweet!" I replied with a hungry grin on my face. "But it doesn't smell like waffles."

She continued down the hall now. "Your father has something special planned for your kill."

I thought to myself, *my kill—what does she mean by that?* And my memory came rushing back to me. I went to my room and took off the diaper and examined the bite on my butt with a mirror. It wasn't that bad. The stitches sort of made a smile shape. I laughed to myself and gingerly pulled on some shorts and a new t-shirt. I hurried up stairs.

Is that you Ben?" yelled my father from the kitchen, knowing that it was me from the heavy thunder of my footsteps.

"Yeah Dad." I tossed my laundry in the alcove in the main floor hallway, where the washer and dryer were.

"Got a plate right here for you—waffles and sausage." Then he laughed a little. "Unless you'd rather have some turtle soup."

I didn't see the humor in that but I did stick my head in the huge stock pot. "There sure is a lot in there."

"He weighed almost forty pounds." My dad patted me on the back. "You sure you don't want some soup?"

"No thanks. I think I'll stick with the waffles." I opened the fridge to get some orange juice and sat down.

"How you feelin?"

"Fine."

"I know how you like waffles."

"You got that wwwite!" My mouth had half of one jammed inside it.

Dad smiled and continued scrambling up some eggs for the rest of the family in a large non-stick pan. I wasn't big on eggs, never had been. When I was one my mom gave me some and I seemed to develop a rash (of course she rushed me to the hospital).

"Honey! Breakfast is ready!" yelled Dad shutting off the stove, and grabbing the toast that had just popped up.

"Coming! Come on, let's go get some breakfast Nancy Sue. We'll finish cleaning up your room later," Mrs. Thompson sat down at the breakfast table overlooking a row of pines which ran through the neighborhood.

"Ding Dong Ding...Ding Dong Ding," rang the front door

bell, followed by a slight creaking of the aging hinges as someone entered.

"Hey Big Country! What's up?" I had my head down on the edge of my plate vacuuming in the last of my food.

"Morning Mr. Thompson—morning Mrs. Thompson," said Wyoming, also known as Big Country to most of the people in town. Legend had it that a few years ago in youth football, there was a fumble on the line of scrimmage in the championship game against Caledonia. The game was tied and Caledonia was on the two yard line—just about to score the winning touchdown. No one really knows what happened. Some say the Center snapped the ball, just as Wyoming let out a loud belch. Others say the noise came from somewhere in his lower extremities, and that the *smell* temporarily dazed the Caledonia players. Well, whatever the case, the Quarterback turned his head just as the ball was snapped and dropped it. Players from both teams dove after it, and it somehow landed in Wyoming's hands. Well, he did what anyone else would do in the same situation. He ran. The Caledonia guys figured out he had the ball, and tried to tackle him. One by one they piled on him, but he stayed on his feet. Legend has it that by the time he crossed the goal line he was dragging the entire team. I guess somebody in the stands said, "That Wyoming looks like he could carry the whole country on his shoulders." Another guy said, "Yeah a big country." After that word spread and the name stuck.

"Want to come play ball with me, Marc, Chondra, and some of the other guys," asked Wyoming, eyeing the sausage in the middle of the table.

"Go ahead." My dad noticed Wyoming ogling over the food."

" No thanks Mr. Thompson, I already ate breakfast…Well,

maybe a couple for a snack. Don't want to run out of energy out there today."

"Can I go Mom?" I was already putting on my shoes.

"Well…, I don't know. I thought I would take you to the doctor just to have you double checked. You gave me such a scare." She was sizing me up. I could tell she was dieing to get me to the doctor. A few weeks ago she rushed me in because I had developed my first couple of pimples. She combed through her 100 pound medical journal and found some rare disease from West Africa and took me to the emergency room.

"Oh Mom—I'm fine." I figured I better get dad involved. "Can I go Dad." He was looking at the paper without really listening. "I guess so."

"Sweet!" I dashed out the door still putting on my shoes.

Mr. Thompson turned to Mrs. Thompson who frowned back at him. "He'll be fine. It'll be good for him to get back with his buddies. I'm just sorry I have to clean up the garage, or I'd go with them."

Mrs. Thompson crossed her arms over her chest and shook her head disapprovingly. "Your father—what are we gonna do with him."

Nancy Sue began to giggle.

# Buckley Poindexter "Oh brother"

The next day a U-haul pulled down our street. One of the most exciting things that happen in a kid's life is when a moving truck pulls up into your neighborhood delivering the newest addition to your microcosm. It is a time of great anticipation—as all the kids peek out through the window from behind the curtains and the safe confines of their home. This is a learned skill. Mother mammals teach this to their young as a means of defense. It's been going on for thousands of years—even before they had curtains. Well anyway, the next step is to sneak out the back door and get a good vantage point from behind your house. Some times it's a good idea to roll up and then un-ravel the garden hose hooked to the spigot on the side of the house. By this point you've usually made your preliminary appraisal of the new kid.

With Buckley—first impressions were conflicting. He started helping his dad carry in boxes—that seemed like a cool thing to do. You could tell it was a strain for him. His arms were like two pieces of rope dangling with knots at the joints.

Basically, he was a walking stick with oversized glasses. On the second trip inside he ran into the doorway with his box, bounced backward like a pinball, stumbled off the landing, and fell into a bunch of rosebushes—ouch.

His little sister busted out laughing at him—they're supportive like that. His dad came out of the garage carrying a plastic tub and looked down at the mosaic of broken antique bottles lying on the sidewalk. "Well—they almost made it to the new house."

Based on this catastrophe Buckley had put himself at the bottom of the social ladder in the neighborhood, and I'm sure he would have stayed there until…

Buckley's mom came out of the house. She was the initial reason I went over there. I don't claim to be able to describe her—but if you took one of those surveys the supermarket magazines do to show you the top ten most beautiful people in the world they would kick all of those so-called beautiful people off the cover and put Mrs. Poindexter on there. She reminded me of the Barbie Dolls my sister use to play with. She doesn't play with them anymore because she has a new hobby—bugging me. Well anyway Mrs. Poindexter looks just like Barbie. I know what you're thinking "Yeah right—sure kid—we believe you." But it's true. She even wears the same outfits. I went and found my sisters collection downstairs in the toy room closet and have matched them all up. I know what else you're thinking. I know—my mom told me the same thing. She said that some scientist took Barbie back to their lab and measured the length of her legs and the size of her chest and everything else and determined it was anatomically impossible for any women to look like Barbie. I thought about this long and hard and came up with a logical answer. The scientists who came to that conclusion—don't get out much.

So Buckley's laying there in a rose bush wrestling and trying to reason with it to let go of his clothes—but I was already on my way over there. It was like I was made of metal and Mrs. Poindexter was the magnet. I probably looked like some fish with a hook in its mouth getting reeled in with his buddies looking at him thinking *what's with him*—except with Mrs. Poindexter there were a lot of lines in the water. I just happened to be the first one caught.

When I arrived in their yard I wasn't sure what to say. The great thing about being a kid though is that it only takes about 5 seconds to make a new best friend. Grown-ups have long since lost that skill. They just stand around talking about the weather and politics even if they could care less about these subjects—then they go home. So I just walked up to Buckley laying there in the bushes and said, "What's up?"

He shuffled his dark rimmed safety-type glasses back onto his nose and looked up at me with a confounded expression. Then he replied, "Uh…the sky," and gave me one of those looks of a fawn in the headlights. I was thinking to my self, *man this kid doesn't have a clue.* I couldn't help but laugh as I reached my hand out to help him up. "You need some help carrying this stuff in?"

"Sure—that'd be great. My mom says as soon as I move all of my possessions inside I can check the neighborhood out for a new species of amphibian."

My first thought was, *look in the mirror kid.* He looked like one of those tree frogs from the rain forest with eyes that bug-out. *This kids gonna need a lot of help.* I said, "That's…cool. I can show you around."

At this point Mrs. Poindexter came out the front door again. "Well. Well. *Who's* your new friend?"

Buckley turned to her, "Hey mom—this is…uh…I didn't get your name." Then he swung back toward me.

Well you can probably guess what I was doing. I was standing there looking like that fish with the hook in his mouth. And my eyes were bugged out of my head like one of those lizards from the rainforest whose eyes are disproportionate for their body.

She just smiled at me and reached out her hand. "I'm Natalie Poindexter."

I stood there—and stood there—and stood there. I always thought when I saw some hokey pokey magician that claimed to hypnotize an audience that it was rigged. But at that moment I was truly hypnotized.

Buckley jabbed me in the side and broke my trance. I'm sure that he had done this before. "I…I…I…—."

"I guess his name is *I…I…I…mom.*"

"How about I just call you *I* for short?" She winked at me.

The next thing I remember was coming out of the trance as an army of All-American boys filled the yard—all with a hook in their mouth. This is the way it played out.

"You need some help moving in?"

"Hey! I was here first!"

"Yeah—but I'm their neighbor."

"I live closer than you do."

"No you don't."

"I can carry more than you."

Take this small sample of dialogue and multiply it by twenty and you can see what happened.

Mrs. Poindexter raised her hand. "Boys boys—why don't you *all* help take Buckley's boxes down to his room. They're marked with his name on them in the back of the U-haul—then you can go play something or show Buckley around."

There was a mad dash to the U-haul which was emptied in one swift motion

A few minutes later we were all down stairs in Buckley's rather organic room.

"These are heavy." Wyoming dropped the three boxes he was carrying.

"Yeah—what you got in these things—rocks or potatoes?!" All of us gave Marc a strange look.

"Why would he have a bunch of potatoes?"

Buckley jumped in, "They're my magazines."

Wyoming opened the top box of the three tubs he carried in. "What kind of crazy comic books are these—Poplar Science, Discovery, Gene-et-ics today—"

"That's Popular Science and Genetics," corrected Buckley.

Everyone turned their heads toward Buckley and then back to Wyoming. Wyoming wasn't exactly the top student in our class but nobody ever corrected him because of his size. We all wanted to see how he was going to react. He looked carefully at Buckley like he was trying to figure out if he should end his existence. If you could picture a giant Troll looking at a Nome with glasses—that's what it looked like.

Marc cut the tension. "*Jumpin jiminy,* Remember when my sister Shar moved down to South Carolina to college? She came back for Christmas break and then had to go back down to school. We took her to the airport. I *had* to carry *her* suitcase for like a *mile* and a *half* because they were remodeling the airport. Well that thing had to weigh about a zillion pounds. I was dragging and pulling. The wheels were squeaking, sweat was rolling down my face like I was sitting in a sauna, and my sister was walking along giggling and texting her friend. All she was carrying was her loaded down purse. So I just stopped dead in my tracks on the concourse.

She looked over at me like I was annoying her by stopping. "What's the matter with you?"

I wiped the sweat out of my eyes and put my hand over my chest to keep it from leaping out. "What do you got in here?! Rocks!!!"

She didn't answer so I pulled open the zipper as cans of corn, beans, and soup started jumpin out along with two ten pound bags of potatoes and some of those huge government size cheese packages my mom buys at Sam's Club—All that was on the floor as people moved around us like we were an island in a stream.

I gazed up at my sister. She just gave me a matter of fact expression and said, "I needed some groceries for school."

I looked back down at the plethora of low priced food rolling around on the floor—39 cent canned corn, 33 cent canned beans, ten pound bags of potatoes, surplus cheese. The whole lot weighed about a gazillion pounds and cost maybe thirty bucks. As much as my sister annoys me, I would have loaned her the money for groceries just to not have to carry that stupid bag. When we went through the scanners the airport security guys stopped her bag three times. I was thinking they were going to holler, *"price check on isle three!"* They kept running it back and forth under the scanner. The security guy who looked like he was trying to smuggle a watermelon in under his shirt called over his supervisor and another guy to study the x-ray image of the contents. They were pointing and scratching their heads. Watermelon guy was reaching for his gun. I started getting nervous. I was thinking, *great—they're going to kill us over some potatoes and beans.* They pulled us to the side and studied us like bugs under a microscope, while the head security guy called in for some backup. A few minutes later two guys in white suits and bullet proof vests with the words, "Bomb Squad" written on them showed up. They studied the scan carefully and slowly opened the bag. The lead guy reached in and pulled out a can of Green Giant. He looked at it with a puzzled expression, glanced over at me with the sweat still rolling down my face, and burst out laughing. The other guys started laughing at me like I was standing there in the middle of the airport naked or something. They could hardly contain themselves as they zipped up the bag and handed it to me. One guy was holding his side to keep his guts from leaping out he was laughing so hard. I looked over at my sister—scowled and trudged down the concourse.

Wyoming was laughing and patting Buckley on the back. A disaster was averted.

"Why you got all these magazines anyway?" Marc asked.

"My mom used to work at Kennedy Space Center—she was a mission coordinator on the Endeavor."

Everyone was opening their boxes. Sure enough most of them had books and magazines.

"I've always had them around since I was little. I kind of learned to read with them," Buckley continued.

Wyoming was looking at a page and trying to sound out a couple of words.

"You mean your mom was on the *space shuttle*?" I asked.

"Yeah," said Buckley rather matter of fact, as if it was no big deal that his mom flew in space.

"Jumpin' jiminy! That's awesome. Did you see her go up?" Marc inquired.

"Kind of—I was only 5. All I remember was it was really deafening."

"What do you mean by that?" Wyoming had an inquisitive gaze.

Marc could sense danger again. "Hey—let's show Buckley the swimin' hole down by the river. Wyoming and I dropped some boards down there this morning so we could make that bench we were talking about."

We took off up the stairs and out the door—pausing disproportionately long to say good-by to Mrs. Poindexter. Each of us personally thanking her for letting us lug in some of Buckley's things.

# Oblivious Animals Take a Drink at the Watering Hole

The first day of high school is tough for any freshman. But if you live in a small town where word spreads faster than butter at a fourth of July picnic, things can be even tougher…

"*Dude*. Pssssttttt. Over here."

"Hey Marc! What's up?"

"Keep it down. Don't you know seniors are lurking the halls to prey on unsuspecting freshman. My older brother told me to keep it on the low down if I intend to survive. He said it was like one of those Wild Kingdom movies with the oblivious animal that's just leaning down at the water hole to get a little drink, and *wham*. *Dude* whatever you do don't use the drinking fountains—and never go to the bathroom unless you want to practice being a fish."

"Come on! It can't be that bad." I gave Marc a look of disbelief and leaned against the lockers. "And how am I supposed to not go to the bathroom all day? You've been watching too much TV."

"Suit yourself. It's your funeral. But if it was me everybody was talking about I wouldn't even have come to school."

"What are you *talking* about?"

"Shhhhhhhhh." Marc pulled me closer like we were in some kind of spy movie. "You know how word gets around fast here. Remember Stanley Pud—something from a few years ago. The dude spilled his apple juice at lunch all over his pants. A few hours later the whole school was saying he peed on himself. Poor guy never lived it down. He had to move a few months later."

"His parents had a job change or something, and they *had* to move."

"That's what they *said.*"

"Ding ding ding ding ding…"

"Crud. We only have two minutes to get to class. You go' in to English Class?"

"Nope. I have Algebra first hour."

"Algebra. That's for the brainee-acs. What you taking that as a freshman for?"

"I like math." I shrugged.

"Who you have?"

"Mr. Farnor."

"Flunk yu Farnor. *Dude,* did *you* ever screw up. He's the *worst* one there is. Whatever you do don't get caught up in any of those foreigner jokes. He'll flunk you for sure. His room's down that hall, last one on the end. See yu Ben, gotta run."

"Thanks Marc." I grabbed my new back pack and dashed down the hall to the last door, ducking in just before the bell.

I scanned the room. Most of the seats were taken. I looked for some friendly eyes. I noticed a couple of cute girls in cheerleading uniforms, but all the chairs near them were taken by guys already. The only open seat was one in the middle of the front row.

Mr. Farnor, a forty-something teacher with salt and pepper hair, a tan sport coat, and a tie with math formulas all over it, came in holding a big cup of Starbucks coffee. "Take a seat people. It's time we got the old motor in your head moving again. I'm sure they're all but seized up from playing X-Box and Playstation Two or Three or whatever all summer. Let's see if we can exercise your brains a little instead of your remote control fingers. How about we have a little quiz to see how much you know." Mr. Farnor gave the class a sly grin, which brought a collective groan from the masses.

"Clear your desks," continued Mr. Farnor, as he walked up and down the aisles passing out his quiz. Once he finished he went to his desk, and reached for his worn leather briefcase with a small combination lock fastened to the side—the kind of lock that tends to keep out only the person who owns it. He fiddled with the four digit code for a couple of minutes trying to get in, then sat down and scratched his Einstein style hair. A few minutes later he was rummaging through his desk looking through hundreds of little yellow Post-It notes for something. Then he blurted out, "Ahh Haa," and began to open his briefcase.

"All right," he muttered to himself. "Let's see who is here."

"Stephanie Anderson"

"Here."

"Susan Belgrits."

"Here."

"Josh Dandruff."

"Present."

A few people chuckled as they looked over their shoulders at Josh dusting off his.

"Robert Gardner... Robert Gardner," repeated Mr. Farnor, looking up through his heavy dark-rimed reading glasses from his seat behind the desk.

"Robert's not here today Mr. Farnor," said a studious looking girl from the first row.

"Thank you Ms. Moore," Mr. Farnor glanced back at his class roster.

"Ben Thompson."

"Here." I looked up at Mr. Farnor quickly.

There was a slight murmuring through the class filled with mostly Juniors and Seniors who had put off taking Advanced Algebra as long as they could. People were leaning over in their seats whispering, some giggled, one finally laughed, causing Mr. Farnor to look up sternly from behind his desk.

"What's all this about. Anyone who talks during my tests will receive a zero, and a trip to the principal's office," said Mr. Farnor scowling at the class, which brought about an immediate silence. I looked over my shoulders to the right and the left. It seemed like everyone was staring at me. I shrunk in my seat.

"Eyes on your own paper people."

\*\*\*

After class I filed my way out of the room back into the hall and pulled out my schedule—second hour World History with Mr. Antiquity. I headed down the hall toward my locker to grab my history book. Unrestrained eyes followed me.

"That's him," said a tall older looking boy wearing a shirt that said **I live for video games.**

I tried not to make eye contact, remembering what Marc had told me that morning about survival. At the time it seemed ridiculous. Marc had a way of exaggerating. But now, as I walked down the white tiled halls, with clean walls that had a hospital sort of feel, I felt like I was being hunted like one of those unsuspecting animals on the Savannah. I picked up the pace trying not to make eye contact with any upper class-men.

"Hey Thompson. Get lost in the woods lately," said a skinny boy with long oily hair and pimples laughing at his own joke.

"I'm sorry about your pet turtle Thompson. You gonna be gone for the funeral this week." said a more athletic looking boy in a condescending voice. Laughter spread from the pack of kids hanging around him.

I reached my locker down the freshman hall and fiddled with the combination. It wouldn't open. I tried again—still no luck. Marc showed up at my side and began twisting his lock. A few seconds later he was inside. I tried pulling up the lock a third time—no luck. I kicked the bottom.

"Chillaxe Dude. What's the problem?" Marc looked over at me trying to ease my frustration. "Those locks take a little practice."

"That's not it." I fidgeted nervously. "They all know I fell out of a tree and the turtle, and everything…"

"I was trying to tell you that this morning. How'd they find out?"

"I don't *know*. It's like you said. Word travels fast."

"Jumpin Jiminy! Do they know about the turtle?"

"Yeah…Woe! Who is that?" My heart had stopped beating.

Marc turned to see what I was looking at, and quickly tried to smile and look cool, as the prettiest girl in the school sashayed by. "Dude you aim too high. That's McKayla Andrews. She's got the Homecoming Queen vote locked and they haven't even nominated or voted yet. You need to just try and *survive the day*." Marc tossed his book in his locker, grabbed his new black high top sneakers and took off. "Later man. I got Gym."

I looked up at the clock. "Thirty seconds til class," I murmured to myself. I gave up on the locker, and dashed down the hall. The bell went off. "Ding ding ding ding." I pulled my scrunched up schedule out of my front jean pocket. Room 207. "Crud," I mumbled.

"No running up the stairs!" yelled a young lady teacher who was closing her door.

At the top of the stairs I slowed down. Scanning the doors I noticed Mr. Antiquity's yellowed placard. The door was already closed. "Crud crud crud." I reached for the worn brass doorknob and opened the door. Everyone's eyes turned toward me. One boy in the back of the room wearing a black concert t-shirt with the word *Panic* in silver letters, leaned over and laughed to his friend, "Lost again." His friend muffled his laugh with his hand and then high-fived his buddy.

"The girl sitting in the middle isle turned in her seat and said, "*Grow up* Zonker."

The boy instantly quieted up. I recognized the girl immediately, (You never forget the first time you fall in love). It was McKayla Andrews. Her hair looked like dark brown silk. Her eyes were huge sapphires positioned perfectly on the most beautiful face I had ever seen. I stood there day dreaming about her, forgetting I was standing in the middle of the room.

"He's so lost he can't even find his seat," coughed the boy named Zonker in the back.

"That's enough Mr. Billsbee," said the man in a Cardigan Sweater with a pipe hanging out of his mouth. "What's your name young man?" I still stood in the front of the room, looking out of place. It probably looked like I was holding up a sign that said, "Look at the idiot."

"Ben Sir. Ben Thompson."

"The lost boy. Yes of course. Well, I trust you can find your seat."

I quickly scanned the room. Two seats were available. One was next to Zonker in the back row. The other was in the middle of the room next to a couple of guys in football jerseys. Neither seat looked very safe. I chose the one in the middle, and sat down quickly. I sunk in my seat wishing I was somewhere else. I would be 15 next week. I had been at high school for just two hours and my life was over. I wondered if I could go to another school. Maybe my parents would move. I felt my confidence sinking and I slouched.

"I'm Mr. Antiquity. And you will have the privilege of having me for World History this semester. I have been teaching World History for a very long time. When I began teaching it was quite fashionable to have a pipe if you were a professor. The Federal Government has mandated that all schools be smoke free, which is fine with me since I haven't smoked in over twenty years. Nasty habit you know. But I got used to having the pipe around. We became sort of attached to each other. Well, anyway. You wont have to worry about me lighting up in here. My friend here, and I quit a long time ago," he said, gesturing at his pipe. "Anyway, I like to get that story out of the way right at the beginning. As for the course, we will examine the major events from the founding of ancient civilizations along river valleys in ancient Egypt, India, China, Mesopotamia, and the ancient cultures of the Americas. Ms. Tyler, can you pass one of these out to each student?"

"Yes Mr. Antiquity."

I felt some little sensation in my head. I thought it was a fly or something. When I brushed the back of my hair three pea size white slobbery globs of paper came out in my hand. I turned my head and saw Zonker twirling a straw like he was some kind of gun slinger or something. His friend next to him was stifling a laugh. I recognized him with the "I live for video games" shirt.

I sunk in my seat as if it were quick sand and tried to make my self invisible. *This was going to be a long day.*

32

# Two of My Fifteen Minutes of Fame

I suited up with the rest of the freshman in the boys' locker room. It was the first week of school but the pungent smell of sweaty socks and stinky jock straps permeated the confines of the locker room. It was like it soaked into the paint in the walls and seeped back out.

Marc was finishing putting on his pads, and sat on the long bench that ran down the middle of each aisle of lockers.

Wyoming, was struggling to pull down his shirt over his gear. "I told them Extra Extra Large, those clowns just gave me an Extra Large." He kept tugging on the bottom of his shirt.

Marc and I decided to help him. Marc yanked down on the front and I gripped the back.

"This is like trying to put a wetsuit on a Walrus." Marc commented as he struggled with the material.

Wyoming leered at his smaller comedic friend.

Marc noticed Wyoming's expression. "I mean a real cool, good looking Walrus."

I burst out laughing and gave up trying to pull the shirt down on Wyoming. Wyoming couldn't help himself and began to chuckle. His shirt only managed to cover his midrib, exposing his hairy stomach which jiggled with the laughter.

Coach Hammer; the varsity coach, came out of his office on his way to the field. He was a rather bulky man sort of shaped like a bullet. He moved a little off balance due to the fact that his right arm was twice the size of his left. He had been in some kind of motorcycle accident when he was a teenager, and his left arm had never healed right. It wasn't the left arm that drew attention from his players though, it was the one that felt like a hammer if you did something wrong. Coach Hammer had been a star quarterback in high school and was expected to take the school to a State Championship until he was in the motorcycle accident. Now as a coach he was still trying to live that down. "You boys came here for fun did you," he growled. His voice had the impact of a lion roaring right in front of you, and stopped our laughter cold. He then walked out of the room onto the field.

"Thanks a lot guys. Now he'll be watching for us to mess up." Wyoming's voice was shaky and unsure.

"Yeah, like he wouldn't notice you anyway," jeered Marc.

"Come on, we better get out there. We don't want to make him any madder."

The three of us made our way out of the Locker room and onto the practice field. Coach Hammer stood with the freshman and J.V. Coaches in the middle of the field. He liked to personally oversee the tryouts to see if there might be a chance of anyone being moved up to varsity.

Coach Hammer nodded to one of his big winded assistants, and the man yelled for all the freshman and sophomores to line up. We all got in line on the fifty. Then Coach Hammer stepped up. "You are the sorriest bunch of sissies I've seen in the last twenty years. But don't worry we'll get you into shape and make you winners." There was a little laughter and agreement from the assistant coaches. "Look across the field at the varsity team. They finished 8-3 last year—One game short of making the playoffs. This year we are picked to win Conference," he paused.

We all looked down the field apprehensively. The varsity looked so much bigger and stronger.

Coach Hammer continued, "You boys are going to get one shot at playing the varsity. Any of you who feel like *peeing* your *little pants* might just as well get off the field right now!"

I thought, *What am I doing? This is crazy.* I knew the other boys must have been thinking the same thing. I could tell by the puddles of sweat forming around their feet even though we hadn't even warmed up yet.

Coach Hammer gazed up and down the line. "Some of you might quit after today! But maybe a couple of you will be bumped up to J.V. and be on your way to girls and glory." He stopped in front of Wyoming and gave him a little nod. Even though it had been several years, Coach Hammer was well aware of the youth football exploits of Wyoming when he carried the whole Caledonia team across the goal line to win the game. "OK boys listen up. You boys who think you're strong enough to play on the line go with Coach Johnson. Running backs go with Coach Tanner. receivers, you're with Coach Manten. quarterbacks, you stay here with me. Now move it!"

"Good luck," said Marc as he trotted off to be with the quarterbacks. I headed over to Coach Manten. One of the varsity receivers came over and walked me and the other prospects through some stretches. Then he ran us through a simple down-and-out pattern that he wanted us all to do. Coach

Hammer yelled, "Let's play ball. His massive senior defense stepped up to the line. "Don't hurt em too bad boys." His seniors chuckled a little. They knew this was going to be fun.

The freshman line crouched. The ball was snapped. "Crunch…ugh…squish…" Four seconds later the freshman line was on its' back along with the first kid to try his hand at quarterback Mike Meyers. The only freshman left standing was Wyoming, who hadn't given up an inch to the senior nose guard. "Wyoming! You move over to center. Lets' see if we can give the next quarterback a chance to throw. Manten! Line up three of those sissy receivers and see if one of them can get open on this play."

Coach Manten pointed to two skinny receivers and then a third one—me. Three defensive backs from the varsity lined up across from us.

Coach handed Marc the ball. "Try not to screw up kid."

Marc crouched behind Wyoming. "Set, 22, 17, 45, hut hut."

The ball was snapped. Wyoming braced himself and held up two varsity lineman for a moment. They bore down on him but he dug in and was planted like a tree in the middle of the field. Marc backed up into the pocket with the ball. It was his turn at quarterback. I took a couple steps to the right and then to the left. The other two receivers were fighting to get free of their defenders. Then I took off with the urgency of a jet on an aircraft carrier runway. My defender ran step for step with me for about ten yards. I made my cut down the sideline pulling away from the defenseman. Marc spotted me in the open—just like we did in our neighborhood games. The ball released from his hand and sailed over all the defenders' heads and landed in my arms as I scooted down the sideline. A couple seconds later I was in the End Zone untouched. I spiked the ball and did a little jiggy dance to a roar of cheers from the freshman.

This was going to be the best day of my life.

Then coach Hammer came storming up to his senior line and the defensive backs. "What are you candy butts doing out here!? You just let a couple of *freshman* burn you." He took a hold of J.D. Nelson's (the guy who was guarding me) shirt with *the hammer arm* and lifted him a couple inches off the ground. He looked like a crazy one arm gorilla holding a rag doll—the rest of us were dead silent and shaking like sycamore saplings in the wind. "If you don't take that freshman out on this play you're setting the bench for the year."

J.D. swallowed hard like he wanted to respond but the words were scared right out of him.

"Do—I—Make—My—Self—Clear!"

J.D. nodded like a bobble head doll.

Coach Hammer set him back on the earth. "Now line the heck up."

I walked over to the line hesitantly. My legs were sticks of butter in the hot September sun.

Marc stepped up to the line behind Wyoming.

Wyoming dug his hoofs into the ground.

I stared across the line at J.D. He was a rabid Pit Bull.

Coach Hammer was yelling, "Kill um!"

A crazy thought ran across my mind in the face of certain death, *I hope U.S. History with coach Hammer isn't this scary.*

Marc yelled, "14, 27, 33, hut, hut!"

I took off down the sideline. J.D. bumped me hard. I stumbled a little but retained my balance. I put my legs into cheetah gear. We were running neck and neck. The ball was released. It looked like it had lots of distance but it wobbled a bit in mid flight. I had plenty of practice catching Marc's passes and I knew this was going to be short. I stopped and turned toward the pigskin. I opened up my arms and watched as it glided in to my chest. I smiled and turned toward the end zone.

Before I could make a complete turn I felt a shooting pain in my side. The ball popped out of my arms. My head jerked like I had been hit by a car. I looked into a pair of angry blue headlights and felt my body being lifted from the ground. I sailed through the air not knowing if I would ever touch the earth again. J.D. came down on top of me and all the air in my body was expelled all at once "Pooooof." I tried to gasp for breath but my lungs didn't work. They were one of those tiny balloons that you can't blow up.

Everything went dark for a few seconds. When I returned from the afterlife I could see Coach Hammer pounding J.D. on the back congratulating him. Then he looked down and said, "Get up Thompson. You're holding up practice."

A minute later the air returned to my lungs and a couple of assistant coaches dragged me to the sideline and tossed me next to the tackle dummies.

I sat there for a while and contemplated my future as a football legend. I was fast but skinny as a rail. My body wasn't made to take much punishment. I decided I would talk to coach Middlebush and see about joining the Cross Country team. Football was great to play in the neighborhood but I was smart enough to know my life expectancy against trained assassins was limited.

It didn't turn out to be the best day of my life but I did have about two minutes of glory with my one touchdown. Buckley said he read once that everyone gets fifteen minutes of fame. I guess I have thirteen left. I figured that was good. No sense in wasting it all at one time.

# Bit by a Bullet

So I started my new sport of Cross Country. At our small school it was not a sensation. The girls' team had about twenty members but the boys' team had only a hand and a half on it and you needed seven for the varsity.

The first day on the team I had no idea what I was getting into. I was sure it would be easier than football because there were no growling, trained, killers. All you had to do was run through some parks and places like that. It sounded simple.

Coach Middleton was excited to have me on the team. He saw me in the annual eighth grade mile run. I finished sixth, but four of the guys that beat me went out for football. The other one was Scarecrow Swanson. He was six feet two inches of straw and weighed about eighty pounds. He was on the Golf team. That left me as the top recruit out of the freshman class.

I strutted into the meeting in the locker room feeling like the number one draft pick on signing day. Coach Middleton gave me a friendly smile, put his arm around my shoulders, and introduced me to the team. I was the only freshman there so I didn't know any of the guys—but I was sure that after today they would all know who I was.

Everyone clapped for me and I sat down. Then he told about the places he went running over the summer and how glad he was to see us all. I always admired coach because he actually ran with us. Once—I had a cool soccer coach who played every step with us. But most coaches stand and yell from the sideline trying to relive their glory days vicariously.

Then coach said something that I didn't understand. "Let's go out and run six."

I looked around as everyone got up and went out into the parking lot to stretch. I just followed along stretching out as some of the guys joked about summer escapades.

"Let's go," said a kid named Bob. He took off running kind of stiff like a robot. I thought to myself, *this guy can't be too good*. I was to find out later that he was the only guy our school sent to state last year—and he won it as a sophomore.

I raced off with the rest of the team. I felt great for about half a mile but kept wondering. *What was the six that coach was talking about? When are we going to stop?*

We approached the corner of Bender Road—the mile mark, and I stopped. Everyone else just kept going. *Where are you going? What is the six?* I leaned over and put my hands on my knees to hold myself up and watched as they all disappeared down a hill.

I started to jog again but felt like I was breathing through a straw and crawled a half mile before I stopped and rested again. I did this two more times and caught one kid who was walking. His name was Todd. He was kind of short and muscular. We walked a while together. He was with the team to train for wrestling but he wasn't much of a runner. He also informed me the six was six miles. I was kind of figuring that out since we were a long way from school.

When we came back to Bender Road where the school was he took off and left me in the dust. I thought to myself *if this guy isn't much of a runner than I must be really terrible.* I arrived at school looking like I had been dragged behind a horse for two hours. Bob was already showered, dressed, and waiting outside. He smiled and clapped when I came into the lot. He was saying something but in my coma-like-state I couldn't focus.

I managed to get home and fall face down on the couch. I found out in the morning that I hadn't moved an inch all day or night. My mom was shaking me. "Get up Ben. You'll be late for practice."

I tried to stand but my legs didn't work and I landed face down on the floor.

"What's that matter honey?" My mom was at my side nursing me. Being the hypochondriac she was she probably thought I had Parkinson's or Cerebral Palsy or something like that.

When you're a teen there's nothing worse than mom loving you. I urged my legs to move but they were like cement blocks. I fell again moaning in agony.

Mom was still babying me. "You better take the day off honey—maybe we should take you to the doctor."

The thought of quitting was jumping around in my head. I had never felt so sore and totally beat up.

Then mom kissed me on the cheek.

That was it! I wasn't gonna have my mom treat me like a baby. I'd been trying to wean her off for the last two years. I forced myself to stand again. Each step was a thousand needles running through my body. I sat down like a ninety year old war vet and had some cereal.

It was then and there in front of a bowl of Cheerios that I made one of the most important decisions of my life. I decided that I was going back to practice.

We ran only four miles the second day. Well—*they* ran four miles. I managed to walk it. By the end I was loosened up enough to jog back into the parking lot and try and look good in front of the girls' team that was finishing their run from another direction.

I came in at the same time as one of the girls. I puffed up my chest and tried to run like a pro. I was smiling like the running was easy.

She smiled back.

That was all it took. There's something sexy about a sweaty girl in running shorts.

My mind was working on something cool to say as we jogged across the lot toward the athletic fields. Good thing girls are better at talking—she broke the ice and we talked all the way into the school. Even sweaty she swelled like a flower garden. It was intoxicating—and in my stupor state my tongue was tied. Lucky for me she liked my smile—and girls are more advanced than boys at this age. I was trying to figure out how to ask her to the movies or something. I also had my mom's voice in my head "look girls in the eye not at their chest." So I strained to keep them looking up. It was a battle. They were almost out of my control. I wanted to yell, "Stop that you fools you're going to blow your chances."

Luckily she sensed I liked her and asked me, "Do you want to see a movie this weekend?"

I just stood there trying to catch flies with my open mouth. *What do I say? What do I say?* "Uh…uh…" I could hear my heart pounding in my ears. My olfactories were in chaos. The sweet smell of her sweat and perfume tossed my brain in a tail spin. "Uh…I—"

"Is that a yes Ben?"

I nodded like some kind of trained pet.

"Great! I'll call you about the time later."

Just like that she was gone

I stood there seeing if I could catch any more flies with my open mouth. I lifted my lower jaw off the floor and stuck it back in its place.

Saturday came like waiting for Christmas when you're six. It was my first big foray into the world of dating and women. And it was a powerful paralyzing force.

I wore a hole through the rug by the door until the bell finally rang. When it did I dashed for cover as if somebody tossed a grenade.

I heard my mom say, "It's nice to meet you Chrissie. Ben's been so excited about your big date."

I about died when I heard that. I hurried from out of the kitchen where I was hiding before mom could say anything else. I tried to look cool and make eye contact but it was hard.

Chrissie was smiling. Her cheeks were full of color.

My mom opened the door for us and gave me her *"what's the matter with you"* look.

A few minutes later we slid into the back seat of the car.

She jabbed me in the shoulder.

"Nice to meet you Mr. Allen," I said.

He reached his huge mitt over the seat. It swallowed my hand. I could hear the bones crushing together. They sounded like walnuts when you take that vice to them.

Chrissie leaned over the seat and handed her dad a C.D.

I tried not to be obvious but I couldn't help it. Her hair was down and she was wearing some short shorts that contoured her body. My mind went blank again.

When she sat back down she was in the middle of the back seat right next to me.

Darius Rucker was playing on the C.D. It was his latest song "All Right." I was thinking to myself that for the first time in my life everything *was* all right.

I put my hand out the window and was grooving it along to the music. Chrissie was doing the same thing in the car—although she looked a lot better.

It was a perfect moment.

Then I felt something hit my hand outside the window. I pulled it in and looked at it. It looked fine. So I started to make little wavy motions again. Chrissie was doing the same. We were perfect together.

I looked up into the review mirror and saw Mr. Allen's eyes staring back at me. I swear his eyes were glowing demon red and foam was coming out of his mouth. I stopped grooving and put my hands on my lap.

Chrissie was still jamming. She reached her silky hand down and put it on top of mine

I screamed. "Ouch!!!!" It felt like a bullet went through my spine. I jumped forward screaming. "Ahhh!!! Help me. Ahhh!!!"

Chrissie looked at me in horror—then grabbed my shoulders. "What's wrong? Don't you like me?"

My body was twisting and contorting. I reached for the door in desperation.

Her dad slammed on the brakes screeching to a halt.

I jumped out pulling at the back of my shirt.

Her dad got out and clutched my clothing. "What is it boy!?"

I was breathing like I was giving birth—in a series of pants. "Something bit me in the spine!"

He pulled up my shirt. "Woaw! I've never seen that kind before. Hold still a minute." He grabbed a pair of tweezers out of the emergency pack from his trunk. "It's still lodged in your skin."

"What is it!?" I demanded. "A bullet—?"

Chrissie gasped.

"A bee," he said like it was a piece of lint or something.

Chrissie looked at my back and laughed.

I felt a tug as if he were pulling a foot long stinger out of my back.

"You're OK now."

I turned expecting to see a bee the size of his fist. I kept looking. I squinted and leaned in closer to his hand. Then I saw it on the tip of the tweezers. I was thinking *this must be a little part of it where is the rest of him?*

He dropped it to the ground. Not that you could see it fall or anything being the size of an atom.

We got back in the car. Chrissie sat up and caught her breath from laughing so hard. "You're *so* funny Ben?

I figured I better play along and pretend I was acting to make her laugh. I remembered Marc's idea about how to get girls. Get them laughing. Maybe he was right about that. Chrissie seemed to be having the time of her life.

When we went into the West End Mall Cinema Chrissie asked me if I knew anything about the film.

When I answered her I sounded like the time I was at the dentist and they numbed my mouth. "Welll why word wit was willy wood."

She started laughin again.

We stepped up to the ticket counter. A young girl sat behind it in her theater vest.

I pulled out my cheap vinyl wallet that I had purchased Friday so I would have one. "wooo wickets wor spwing bwake wee wees."

The ticket girl scrunched up her nose and rolled her eyes.

Chrissie giggled some more and grabbed my arm. My whole body seemed to be swelling with confidence.

We walked to the snack counter. As we made our way there people seemed to be staring at us. I thought to myself *we must look pretty good.*

I got to the front of the line.

A Pimple faced boy behind the counter looked at me then acted like he was going to be sick.

I figured *he better take it a little easier on the popcorn.*

I placed my order. "Won warge wombo wees."

Chrissie looked over at me. "Oh my god Ben!"

"What, what?"

She covered her mouth with her hand. "Your face is swelling like a balloon."

"Wy fwace wiz what?"

"It must have been the bee," she observed.

I looked into the shiny surface on the back of the popcorn machine and saw the Elephant Man wearing my clothes.

The next thing I remember were a few fuzzy images flashing through my mind and those same two ambulance people looking down at me and talking to me on a first name basis. That was my one and only date with Chrissie Allen.

# Whoops

As I already have mentioned. There are a few things that run through a boys mind at age 14. Mostly it's girls.

Other things are: What am I going to be when I grow up? And, is my mustache coming in?

Really I don't have any idea what I want to do when I grow up. I used to think I would be a doctor. It seemed like the easiest thing to do—except for all the smoking. You see when I was eight we were always heading to school or practice. When we loaded into the car I would look out the window and see my neighbor standing out on the stoop.

I asked my mom, "Why does Mr. Elton always stand out on the porch wearing his pajamas?"

She laughed and said, "He works in a hospital."

That made sense to me because he was always standing out there smoking like a chimney. I figured he thought he au'ta be at the hospital in case he was having trouble breathing. Plus it would make sense if he got in good with the other doctors for when the time came. He would stand there rain or shine, winter or summer. He'd smoke and cough and suck in some more smoke and cough again. I figured that wasn't very smart. So if they gave this guy a doctor's certificate—they must be easy to get.

It was later that I learned it took ten years to become a doctor. The idea of staying in school an extra ten years to a 14 year old kid isn't very appealing. Plus I think there is a better way. I was reading that a long time ago people didn't go to medical school. They just learned how to be a doctor from another doctor. You went and hung out with him at the office for a while and watched what he did. After a while you knew everything you needed to know. They still do this for electricians and plumbers. I asked my dad why they still didn't do that for doctors. He said, "Politics." That's his standard answer for most questions.

Well, anyway I'm not sure what I want to do. Maybe be a millionaire for inventing something useful like a special kind of foot spray or a toothbrush that senses if you cleaned your teeth enough. I watched enough commercials to know how to do this. You market it for $19.95 and give them a second one for free if they call in the next ten minutes. It's pretty easy. So I might do that. My interest in science has been going up lately since Mrs. Poindexter moved across the street. So I might do that for a living. Who knows?

Off course looking good—or at least believing you look good at 14 is important. So after I survived by first two weeks of school and people forgot all about me getting knocked out and being missing for half a day over Labor Day break, I figured things would get better. And since Chrissie Allen decided to be just friends I figured I needed a new image.

I wasn't hiding out as much and I had almost forgotten about Marc's Wild Kingdom analogy. But when girls started giggle when I strolled by trying to look cool, I figured it was time to get the doo done.

I asked Marc in the hall at school. "What do you think of my hair?"

He smirked then busted out laughing like it was the funniest question he ever heard.

"Thanks a lot." I said.

He gathered his composure for a second. "Well Einstein, It looks like an unkempt bird nest. I keep wonderin' when I'm gonna' see them Warblers hatch you got nestin' up in there."

When I got home I told mom I needed a hair cut.

She looked at me with this *I told you so* look. "I'll take you down to the barber shop after Nancy-Sue gets off the bus."

When we got there I should have read the signs. But boys aren't always that perceptive. There are two places a guy doesn't want to hear the word "whoops" one is at the doctors—especially if you're having a vasectomy. The second is at the barber shop. The first sign that I should have walked out were all the people waiting. Later the second sign should have been that the barber was complaining about his scissors being too dull. The third sign was that he stopped twice to put on a band-aid. But—like I said, boys aren't always that perceptive.

So I watched him reach out his bloody hand and take the man's money that was in the chair before me. He wiped his face with his shirt sleeve and looked over at me. "You ready fella?"

He was a real burly looking barber. I bet he was a big football player back in the 1800's. He looked all grumpy; like he missed his big break and was stuck there cutting hair. I was guessing this was his fall back plan for his original fall back plan.

He brushed all the gray gnarled hair off the chair and looked at me with this *move it or lose it look.*

I sat down in the saggy brown leather barber chair. I

wondered *how many people have sat in this chair.* I sat back
and he pumped the peddle and jerked me up in the air a few
inches.

"What'll it be kid?" His voice sounded like he had gravel in
his throat.

"Uh…uh…just a trim sir."

I heard him grumble something about the amount of hair I
had and how I was going to give him Carpel Tunnel. I'm not
sure what that is. But I was pretty sure I didn't have it so I knew
he wouldn't catch it from me. I did have Lice once back in fourth
grade. That was a big pain. My mom made us put Mayonnaise
in our hair every night for a month. And we had to wear these
old lady shower caps every night. What a pain.

The grumpy barber of Seville was hacking away at my hair.
I heard him mumble something about needing his special
clippers. I got one glimpse of them in the mirror. They looked
like the hedge trimmers my dad uses in the yard.

I sat there as my hair came showering down upon me. I
looked up in the mirror for a moment and saw a gleam in the
barber's eye. I wasn't sure but I think he was making topiary
with my head.

Then I heard the sound that all men fear.

"Whoops!"

I jerked my head up and saw a lump of sod hit the floor. Then
felt a warm liquid run down my forehead. I ran my hand across
it. It was covered in red liquid. I started to feel real dizzy.

I awoke a little while later. Those same two ambulance
drivers were standing over me.

The big guy was running this container of smelling salts
under my nose to revive me. "You OK Ben?"

I coughed a couple times. I didn't have the heart to tell him the smelling salts weren't necessary—the Aqua Velva that the barber painted on was more than strong enough. My dad has some on his work bench. Someone gave it to him for Christmas back in the 1800's. He uses it to get the rust off of bolts and screws and stuff like that.

I coughed again and sat up.

My mom was all frazzled as usual, "Oh my baby! Are you all right?" She put her arms around me and patted me on the head.

"Ouch! That hurt."

"Sorry honey—I thought I lost you."

Now I finally realized where I was. And the only thing that came to my mind was, *not again.* There was no way I could keep this quiet. There is one location you never go if you want to keep a secret—and that's a hair cut place. They are the biggest rumor mills on the planet. People had finally stopped talking about me and calling me "the lost boy." Now it would start all over again. What would they call me this time—Barber Boy Ben?

I looked pleadingly at my mom, "can we move?"

The Med Tech helped me up to my feet and led me and my mom out past the twirling red and white sign. I looked over at the barber. He was sweating bullets. I could tell he was worried about being sued. His other customers nervously got out of their chairs and made their way to the door. The second medical person went over to the barber. "You're running a fever," she said.

I felt sorry for the guy. He was working even though he was sick—probably needed the money to feed his family. I put my hand on the door frame as we were leaving. "I know it was an accident mister. I hope you have a good day."

We left in the car. I could still see him in the window. He smiled at me. I was glad. I didn't want some out of work burley ex football player walking around town with a pair of clippers looking for me. I had enough problems of my own—like finding a hat big enough to cover my head.

When we got home mom cut the rest of my hair. It looked OK from one side. When I turned the other way there was a big divot. A divot is a hole you make on a golf course when you swing. My friend Wyoming is real good at making them.

I went to bed wondering if that Miracle Grow Hair Tonic I saw on TV really works. I made a mental note to ask mom if we could buy some in the morning.

That night I had the worst dream ever about being the only bald kid in the high school. And in the dream Alabama Jackson came up to me and was being all nice. He said, "sorry about the way I been pickin' on yu'. Why don't yu let me take yu out fer some fun."

I went with him and a bunch of his buddies down to the Village Lanes—the local bowling alley.

I got my shoes and found a ball. "This is great Alabama."

He smiled at me. "Yeah! I always knew you and me was gonna be real close."

His bud's all laughed together.

"Why don't yuall' go first."

I went up and took a crack at it. I got a seven on my first throw and almost picked up my spare.

"Good try," said Alabama.

All his bud's laughed together again.

My next frame I got a big split.

Alabama got up and came over to me on the lane. "Why don't I show yu how to do dat." He walked up all smile'in and jabbed one of his henchmen in the side with this "watch this" look on his face. Then he grabbed my balled head like it was a bowling ball. He stuck his thumb in my mouth and two fingers up my nose and proceeded to drag me up to the approach. Then he did his four step release and sent me sailing down the lane.

My hands groped at the oily lane to slow myself down but it was impossible to get a hold of anything. I slid right into the pocket head first for a perfect strike. After the pins settled I gazed back down the alley.

Alabama was yucking it up with his buds.

Then the machine dropped the sweeper thingy that dragged me back in the depths of the alley where no one is supposed to see. Then my shirt became caught in this tumbler thingy that began suckin me into the abyss. I kicked and squirmed trying to get out of my shirt.

I woke up in a cold sweat screaming. In my dark room I couldn't tell if I was out of the ball return tunnel or not. When I finally came to my senses I stumbled to the bathroom and tossed some cold water on my face. I was sure that nothing could be as bad as the nightmare I just had. But I had no idea how wrong I was.

# Mom and Dad drop the bomb

My sister Nancy-Sue was gone to a friend's house for the weekend. And after having as many things go wrong as I did the first few weeks of school I was glad to have the house to myself.

Mom made my favorite—Lasagna. She has the best recipe in the world. It was handed down from my great grandma. If you think you've had great lasagna before you have no idea. Back before my dad went to work writing for the Grand Rapids Press we use to live in Florida. Mom and dad had a restaurant called The Sea Island Café. It was on this main road going out to Folly Beach. Dad started it from scratch. He had been managing a couple of businesses for other people but got tired of that. He was working all the time and the owners were making all the money. So mom and dad rented this old house on the side of the main road out to the beach and converted it to a cool café. They had a jammin business. Dad says they were turning people away every day. But I guess it took a lot of time to run so dad sold it when I was born and went back to college for his masters in journalism.

Anyway dad had other chef's and the food critic raving about his lasagna recipe. The food critic for the paper down there said, "If I was going to die and could only have one last meal that would be it."

Mom also made my favorite dessert cheesecake. She'd only made this for me two times before in my life. Once was for my tenth birthday because I kept bugging her ten times a day for weeks on end. The second time was for a big Christmas dinner we had at our house with about twenty of our relatives. It was really crowded. We were packed inside like sardines. Everybody kept bumping into each other like we were in that bumper car thing at the fair.

My aunt Shelly said, "Isn't this so cozy."

"Yea...*real cozy!*" replied my uncle Don who was drinking wine. "It's about as cozy as a prison cell full of nut jobs."

Everyone laughed but you could tell that most of them agreed with uncle Don. Our house was just too small to have that many people.

My dad summed it up best when everyone left. "It's nice having all the family together but families get along better when they're not *too* together."

That was the last time I had homemade cheese cake.

I sat down at the kitchen table.

"Do you want some ice cream with that?" Mom inquired warily.

"Yeah sure."

Like I said before teenagers aren't that perceptive. I should have picked up that something wasn't right. But instead I just had that deer in the headlights glaze in my eyes as I attacked my double slice of cheesecake.

Mom and dad sat in the chairs on both sides of me. I was almost finished when I noticed that they hadn't taken a bite and their ice cream was making a milky lake around their cheesecake.

Then I looked up and I swear I heard that music they play in movies where the guy on death row is heading for the chair.

I stopped chewing. The cheesecake was stuck on the roof of my mouth.

Dad looked at mom with a look of hesitation. Then he turned back to me.

I could hear that music again in my head.

"There's something we have to tell you Ben," Dad managed to say before he had to take a drink of water.

I was thinking, *Oh no! What is it? Did dad lose his job and we have to move? Did Grandpa die?* I should have been thinking *why did he call me Ben? He usually calls me son.*

Dad swallowed like he was trying to swallow a mouth full of screws. "Son, you know we love you."

My eyes were bugging out of my head like a rain forest frog.

"We love you more than anything in the world."

I thought, *Oh crud.*

Dad swallowed another mouth full of nails. "There's something we need you to know." He paused like he needed an oxygen tank or something. "We've been waiting until you were old enough to understand. We just never knew when we should tell you this."

I thought, *Oh crud, Oh crud!*

Dad swallowed more screws. "Son—you're..."

Mom intervened, "Ben—we adopted you."

The words passed through me and out the other side. I just went back to finishing my cheesecake.

"Ben—we thought we would tell you when you were younger but we just never could..." My dad looked like he was going to cry. "We just thought you were too young...or the time never seemed right."

I scraped my plate for the last drop of cheesecake. I looked up and smiled. Mom was staring at me waiting for some kind of reaction. I asked, "can I go play my Play Station?"

Dad didn't know what to say. "Uh...sure Ben."

I took off down stairs.

Dad and mom sat in the table in shock. "That's not how I pictured this going."

"Me neither," Mom replied.

In my room I started to play NCAA Football 2009. It was the middle of the first quarter when I dropped the controller. What they had said to me had boomeranged back into my brain and stuck like the cheesecake. I moved from denial to anger. *Why didn't they tell me this before? How could they keep this from me? On top of how crummy this year has gone—now they dump this on me. I hate them!*

It was a week later after walking around like a lit firecracker ready to explode that I finally sat down to get some facts from mom.

She started all teary eyed. She can cry during a cartoon movie so this had her falling to pieces. "Your father and I were living on Johns Island down in Florida. He was tired of working for everyone else and we opened the restaurant. I was almost thirty and we had been wanting a baby for a long time." She gazed out the window of my room. She seemed to be looking all the way to Florida. "I never told you this before but I was pregnant twice before you were born. Twice I carried a boy. Once for six months and the second time all the way but they were both still-born." Her watery eyes peered back at me. "They said it was likely I could never carry a child. I was *crushed* Ben.

I wanted a baby *so* bad. I walked around in a half life like state for months. Your father was *really* worried about me. Then it seemed like fate. A woman who was one of our regulars came in with a new baby boy. Your father knew she hadn't been pregnant so he asked whose baby it was and she explained she was with the Cook County Adoption Agency. She told your father, "I'm one of the supervisors there. We take the kids out with us as much as possible. They don't need to be locked up all day. The children need to get some fresh air—this baby is so cute I wish he was mine."

Your father looked at that baby and thought about me. Later that day we went down to the agency. He was right. I fell in love with you instantly. It wasn't the best timing with having a new restaurant and all but we started the paper work and a couple months later you came home with us. You were the cutest baby." She grabbed my cheeks. "You still are the cutest."

"*Mom,*" I said pulling her hands off my face.

She started to cry again.

I put my arms around her back and hugged her.

"Now I worry you won't love us as much any more." She sobbed in my shirt.

My anger at mom was gone. But an inner rage with whoever was my real mom replaced it. "You're my mom. You raised me." I patted her on the shoulders.

She grabbed me hard and squeezed the air out of me.

I decided I couldn't be mad at mom and dad for falling in love with me and adopting me. I was a little upset that they waited until I started high school to tell me. But I guess there is never a good time to tell someone that they are different. Off course I kind of knew I was different—no one in the family had as many accidents happen to them as I did. Now I had to try to find out who my real parents were. That way I would know who exactly to be mad at.

# The Library

The creaking continued down the stairs. Then a familiar voice rang out.

"Ben. You down here?"

"Hey Marc. What you up to?"

"I thought I'd come over and help you out with that new snow boarding game on your Play Station."

"That was *real thoughtful* of you," I said in a condescending tone.

"Well you know me, always looking out for others." Marc grinned, and grabbed the controller for the PS2. "Say, you never told me what McKayla Andrews said. I can't believe you just walked up and talked to the Diva of the school. Come on. What did she say?"

I blushed a little. "I asked her to homecoming."

"Are you crazy! She's going to be the homecoming queen. She'll probably go with Chase (Rocket Arm) Jerkowski. He's the senior quarterback. quarterbacks always win homecoming king."

"That doesn't mean they have to go together."

"Know they don't *have to* go together. But why would a senior girl want to go to homecoming with a freshman. You can't even *drive*. What you gonna do, pick her up with your *bike*. *Oh yea*, I can see it now, her in her fancy dress riding on your handlebars. Or maybe you could have your *mom* drive you. *That would be cool*." Marc began to laugh at his own jokes.

I scratched my sandy brown hair and tossed the small basketball into a tub containing a few light sabers, various balls, game controllers, and other miscellaneous boy essentials. He plopped down on the oversized beanbag in front of the TV.

"So—what did she say."

I hesitated a moment and told him, "she said she'd think about it."

"Wait till Rocket Arm hears about that—he'll kill you."

I sat there in a daze for a moment. I hadn't let anyone know what my mom told me about being adopted. I kept thinking it was some kind of bad dream like the bowling alley one. This whole high school thing hadn't turned out like I had planned. What I had to do was find out who my mom was. Then I would know who to blame for all my bad luck. "Marc. Do you want to go to the library?"

"Are you OK? Did that barber take out some of your brains? It's Saturday. *No one* goes to the Library." Marc was squeezing the buttons on the controller for the PS2, not taking his eye off his game character, who was flying down a snowboarding run through a strange neon cluttered city in the mountains. He jerked from side to side as if he were dodging the obstacles the character in the game faced. I grabbed the bandaged spot on the top of my head. "You don't *have to* go. I just want to do some research." My voice was a little testy.

Marc pushed the pause button on the controller. "You don't

have to get worked up. I'll go with you. Maybe there will be some egg head girls hanging out there, and I can put the old Marc moves on them."

"Yea, they'll never know what hit them." I Laughed, as I flipped off the game and headed out the room.

Marc followed me up the stairs. "Hey what you gonna research anyway?"

"Genealogy." I sat on the slate floor and put on my Starberrys.

"Genealogy—I never knew you were so interested in blue jeans." Marc grinned. "That sounds cool."

Mrs. Thompson hollered from down the hall as she put in another load in the endless cycle of laundry. "Where you going Ben?"

"Marc and I are going to the Library." I made my way to the door. "Be back in a couple hours."

"Be home for dinner," said Mrs Thompson as she heard the door shut and realized the boys were already gone.

The community Library was in an old stone building off of main street. It had once been the home of one of the town's early settlers. The family had donated it to the community.

Ben and Marc made their way up the flower lined walkway that led from the sidewalk to the entrance. They passed the green historic marker sign that stood in the front yard testifying to the buildings significance.

"I don't know why they bother to put those green signs in front of all these old houses like this. Everyone knows it's old. Who needs a sign to tell them that?" Marc entered the huge double door entryway. "People must have been bigger in the past. Look at the size of these doors."

"Actually people used to be smaller hundreds of years ago,"

I told him while pulling the door closed behind us. "Look at my Grandma. She's about five foot even. I was taller than her in 6<sup>th</sup> grade. And my Grandpa Thompson, he's only about five-nine, even though he claims he used to be five-eleven. He says he's shrinking."

Marc laughed.

"Sh…sh…shh…" said the Librarian from behind the long dark polished wood counter. She glared down at us through her heavy rimed square black spectacles. "You boys use your Library Voice," she shushed, and returned to logging in returned books.

Marc whispered over to me, "Why do all librarians look the same? It must be part of their training program. I can see it now. Question one do you wear old school glasses? Question two can you say Shhhhhhhhh."

I snickered at Marc's comedy routine, and the Librarian again hushed us, "Shhhhhhhhhh"

I walked up to the counter.

She looked up from a stack of books in front of her. "Can I help you young man?"

I'm interested in some books on Genealogy.

The Librarian peered down the top half of her bifocals at me.

"Do you want some information about the genealogy of famous people or about how to search your family tree."

"That's not exactly what I was looking for…I'd like to find out…how someone would find out who their parents are."

She seemed a little more intrigued by my questions. She took off her glasses and rubbed them on her librarian style shirt. "You mean you don't know who your parents are?"

I looked around to make sure no one was too close. "That's right maam."

"Well…I don't think there is much you could find in any book. If you knew where you were born you could search the newspaper archives and maybe find a birth announcement. Or you could try to search on line." She seemed saddened by the topic.

Marc came up to the counter.

I said "thank you," and headed back to the archive section in the dusty corner and began to look at the titles on the old wooden shelves. Marc looked at the titles and read them off to me.

"What are we looking for exactly?" asked Marc. "How about this one, *Germs: your friend.*"

"That sounds good," I said, not paying any attention as I shuffled through the shelf.

Marc could tell that I wasn't listening so he sat the book down on the table next to the bookcase. "I'm going to see if there are any girls here," and he walked off. "That sounds good," I said, engrossed in the book I found about Genetics. The problem was that I couldn't understand everything in the book. I needed a translator—Somebody who was good at reading scientific stuff.

I heard the Librarian say "Shhhhhhh" and looked up to see who she was quieting down. Not to my surprise it was Marc, who had found a girl in the section with headphones and CD's. Marc was trying to get her attention by making fart noises with his hand under his armpit.

I grabbed the book about Genetics and another one about DNA and made my way to the check out counter. I motioned for Marc. He smiled at the girl with headphones and dashed out the door with me.

"What's your hurry? I had her eating out of my hands."

"I don't think anyone would want to eat out of *those hands* once they've been under your armpit making farting noises," I laughed.

"That was a figure of speech. I had her laughing. I read in Cosmo one time in the doctors' waiting room, that the quality girls like most in guys they meet is being funny."

"Yeah, but I think there is a difference if they're laughing *with you* or *at you.*"

"*What ever*," snapped Marc rather sarcastically. "What books did you check out?"

I pointed to the leather bound covers.

Marc shook his head back and forth. "Jumpin jiminy! I'm really worried about you."

On the way back I picked up a thin Maple branch that was lying on the edge of the sidewalk and began to drag it along. It made a "SSSSSSSS Bump" sound as it hit the seems in the sidewalk. "Why are you interested in that stuff anyway? Marc inquired in an unconcerned way.

Marc was my friend but I didn't want anyone to know about this yet. I had enough problems already. I wanted to track these people down that abandoned me and meet them face to face and give them a piece of my mind.

# Homecoming dance

The fall was moving along like syrup through a straw. It was the middle of October and my bald spot was filling in. Most people just snickered slightly when they saw me. Zonker still pointed at me and tried to come up with something smart to say. He always failed but it still made me feel like crap.

Of course you can probably guess that McKayla Andrews never gave me an answer about going to Homecoming. Once and a while I would see her in the hall sashaying by in her cheerleading uniform—Her long hair flowing like one of those models on TV with the fan blowing on them.

I got up enough nerve to ask her three times. It usually went something like this.

Me: "Uh...hi...McKayla." I would sometimes look at her or at my shoes. "I was wondering if you decided if you would go with me to the dance?"

Her friends would giggle like geese.

Then she would say, "No. I'm still thinking about it Ben." And she would wink at me.

At first I thought this was a way of flirting. I told you teenage boys just aren't that perceptive. I came to realize that the laughter I heard each time I left was at my expense. Marc was right. Why would she want to go to Homecoming and ride on the handle bars of my bike? What was I thinking? It made me feel like a marionette and she was just playing me like the puppet master.

Buckley came over the night of the dance. He would have looked pretty good at the Braille institute dance. His light brown hair looked neat. I could tell his mom had a hand in fixing him up—and she was an expert in that. He was sporting some contact lenses instead of his heavy black rimmed glasses. I could tell he had run back to his room at the last minute and changed his pants because they were three inches too short. His mom would have never approved of those.

I sat on my bed studying a computer printout on genetics trying to figure out what all the symbols meant.

Buckley walked in "You goin' to the dance in those duds."

He sounded like some guy from the fifties. I was guessing this was his first dance and he probably read a manual about it or something. I put the printout on my pillow. "Nope! I'm not goin'."

He looked at me in shock. "What do you mean you're not going? You've been telling me I needed to go since I met you."

I got off the bed and turned on my TV. "I got better things to do." I sat on the edge of the bed with my feet up on the frame.

"He sat down next to me. "I can see you're *real* busy." He grabbed me with both arms and shook me. "Are you insane? There's going to be 200 girls there."

"I have some work to do."

He picked up the papers off my pillow. "What you working on DNA for?"

I reached over and cleaved them out of his hand. Then a light bulb went off in my head. "Can you read these papers?"

"Sure. It's pretty simple. They use all this in forensic science. I've been reading this since I was six.

I was thinking, *if I have Buckley help me with this I might have a chance of finding my mom. Buckley's the perfect assistant he's kind of an idiot-genius. He can figure out all the information but he won't have a clue why he's doing it.* "Buckley, do you think you could help me with this research project I have?"

"Sure," he said while switching off the TV. "You just have to go to the dance with me. I need somebody to coach me so I can make all the *right* moves."

I was thinking about the irony of the situation. I was at the bottom of the high school social ladder and Buckley wanted me to coach him. "All right," I caved in. "Give me a few minutes to get ready." I tossed on some jeans with holes in the knee and a solid black t-shirt.

"Is that what you're wearing?" Buckley was laughing to himself.

As unpopular as I was I knew I was closer to cool in my holey jeans then he was in his floods.

When we wheeled up to the door on our bikes Buckley's hair was sticking out all over like he had been electrified. Mine wasn't as bad since it was so short. Mom had cut it herself to match the patch the barber had hacked off, which now looked like a putting green. I couldn't build up enough nerve to go get my hair cut again. I was thinking of letting it grow out like Repunzel although I didn't think anyone would come to my rescue.

The dance was in full swing when we arrived. Green and

white balloons were all over the floor—those were Wildcat colors. A reflective disco ball hung from the cafeteria ceiling and bounced off light in all directions.

Buckley and I worked our way along the edge to a place where a few of the other freshman boys were standing.

The D.J. was mixing up some Funk with a little Michael Jackson tossed in. The dance floor was packed

Buckley tapped my shoulder. "Who should I ask to dance?" Then he blasted some breath freshener in his mouth.

We scanned around the room timing it with the flashes of light from the strobe. On the dance floor there were a few couples. I spotted McKayla and Rocket-Arm dancing together. McKayla was laughing like she was having the time of her life. And Rocket-Arm was as smooth on the dance floor as he was on the football field—which made me like him even less. I didn't recognize any of the other couples out there which probably meant they were juniors or seniors. The other fifty people out on the floor were all girls dancing with their friends.

Buckley leaned in to me again. "This is my first experience with this ritual. It is very interesting that the girls go out together and gyrate their bodies in a seductive manner with the other girls. It's the same thing with the Mojimbo tribe in Africa. The women cause great arousal in the young men as they dance around the fire. The men watch as the women become fatigued one by one. Once they are weakened by all the dancing the men overpower the women. Is that what we do here?"

A small chuckle came out of me. Then I thought about it for a second. Basically he was right. "Let's go to the punch table. We might be able to start a conversation over there." I couldn't hear his reply over all the music but he followed me to the punch. A few parents and teacher chaperones were behind the table. They were the ones who knew what went on at these dances and that was why they volunteered to chaperone. I always figured the chaperones were the wildest kids at their party's years ago. It's ironic that adults always say how much fun they had in school but never want kids to do the same things. Take Mr. Johnson for example. He's always saying in class, "high school was the best time of my life." But there he was cutting in on some kids dancing *too close* together. How can you slow dance three feet apart? It doesn't work.

I spotted a possible match-up for Buckley. Patty Dornhauser was standing by herself at the end of the punch table. I didn't recognize her at first. She normally wore horned rimed glasses and old style skirts and lived in the library during recess. She was wearing a nice dress which revealed she was definitely a girl. I have to admit she looked pretty good. "Buckley. Go over and ask Patty to dance."

He looked at me with his confused look. "How do I do that?"

I could tell his heart was racing. He had the same look when we got our first report card a couple weeks ago. He was so worked up that he might get one A-. Of course he didn't. I had done pretty well my self. It's amazing how much study time you get when you're unpopular.

"Buck—just go over and ask her."

He scratched his head. "What do I say?"

C walked up to us. She was wearing a red and white striped shirt and some blue jean Capri's. "Hi guys. How's it going?"

"I was about to show Buckley how to go talk to Patty."

"Oh—this should be good." She smirked.

I turned my attention back to Buckley. "Walk over there real cool like. But don't look at her. Pretend you don't notice her." I grabbed his shoulders to make sure he was paying attention to me. "Then look at your watch like you have an important appointment. Make sure she notices. Then turn toward her and say, "I don't have a lot of time—but would you like to trip the light fantastic."

C started to laugh and coughed up some of her punch. "Are you *serious*?" She wiped the drops of red liquid off her face. "Where did you learn something like *that*! Girls don't respond to that."

"It was in a movie I—."

She cut me off. "A movie—*oh brother.*"

I put my arms on my hips. "Well if you have such great advice then you tell him how to do it." I didn't like being shown up in front of Buckley.

C started to school Buckley in the art of conversation.

I just stood there and listened. As PO'd as I was about being laughed at I was interested in what she had to say since she was kind of a girl and all.

"Buckley. It's real easy. Don't make it work. Just walk over there normal like and go right straight up to her. Look her in the eyes and tell her she looks really nice and ask her if she would like to dance."

I was thinking to my self, *that can't work. That's too easy.*

Buckley looked at me and then C. He slammed his punch like a shot of whisky, wiped off his chin with his sleeve, and handed C his empty cup. Then he started walking over to Patty with robotic smoothness.

C and I looked at each other and smirked.

Buckley stood a couple of feet from Patty. Then he looked at his wrist as if he was looking at his watch—even though he didn't have one.

C rolled her eyes. "I guess we know whose advice he decided to take."

I smiled and mumbled under my breath, "Go get her Buckley," and gave an approving nod.

Patty noticed Buckley looking at his arm and asked, "What's the matter with your arm?"

He turned to her. He hadn't practice anything for this response. He looked over at us like a child looking for his mommy.

C nodded her head at him and mouthed the words she had told him to use.

Patty asked, "who you looking at?"

He turned toward her.

I could tell he was nervous. He looked like he was about to pass out.

The song ended and a slow love song called "Beth" from a band named Kiss came on.

Buckley turned back to C.

She nodded at him.

Then he swung toward Patty and started to say something. She smiled at him and nodded her head yes.

I turned and gave C the thumbs up. We smiled together. It was a long quiet moment. Then we heard a scream. We spun our heads to see what all the commotion was about.

Buckley was lying flat on the floor on his back. Patty was leaning over him with her face right up to his. "Are you OK Buckley."

Mr. Johnson raced over and knelt down to see what was going on, and Patty stepped back. He sniffed Buckley like he expected to smell alcohol. Once he discovered there would be no "big bust" he shook Buckley. "Get up boy! What's the matter with you?"

The music stopped and the whole school was looking at Mr. Johnson helping Buckley to his feet. Some kids pointed and laughed, others whispered with their friends.

C ran over to check on him.

I stayed back. For once—everyone wasn't looking at me.

# Attack of the texting zombies

I was watching this scary movie the other night. My friend Marc was staying over and my mom let us stay up later because it was a Friday night.

We made some popcorn and were settling down in the family room—which was cool because that meant my pesky sister Nancy-Sue had to leave us alone. Of course she didn't. She kept peeking in on us and doing cartwheels in front of the T.V. She can be soooo annoying.

Mom brought us down two extra pepperoni pizzas and some chocolate smoothies. I think she felt bad for me because of the hair cut.

"Jumpin Jiminy! This is sweet," Marc was sucking down his smoothie. "You *sure* live it up around here."

I stared at him shaking my head with this oh brother look. "It's not like this every night. My mom just feels sorry for me after falling out of the tree and almost dieing and then being scalped like some dude in an old western."

Marc laughed. "Yeah you sure had a smooth start to school."

I popped another piece of pepperoni pizza in my mouth. "See if you can find another show."

Marc leaned back on the couch and grabbed his gut. "I'm *too* full. I don't think I can reach the remote." He's such a ham.

I groaned a little. "Come on man. It's closer to you."

Marc gazed down at the coffee table and kicked his left foot. The remote slid over to my end of the couch. "No it's not. It's *way* closer to you." He started laughing and then grabbed his side. "Don't make me laugh I'm too full."

I tried to grab the remote with my feet but dropped it twice. Finally I groaned like I was giving birth and sat up. "I don't see how women can carry a whole baby. I feel like a stuffed Thanksgiving turkey." I leaned over my bulging belly and snatched the remote. I found a Seinfeld show. That didn't work though because it made us both laugh, which hurt. I switched the station and found this old black and white movie with creepy organ music and we each settled onto our air mattresses on the floor. There was a guy in the movie who was an archaeologist and he had this nice looking assistant. They crept through an old dusty pyramid with these torches that kept going out. There were snakes and all sorts of prehistoric size insects down there. When they reached the inner sanctum they came across this golden sarcophagus covered with dust. The organ music picked up so I knew something was about to happen. The archaeologist studied the writing on the tomb and read it out loud. "He who disturbs the dead shall suffer a—that's all it says. Part of the writing is broken off." He then turned to his assistance and said, "Let's see what's inside."

Marc and I were looking in disbelief.

"What are you doing you idiot. That's a bad idea," I pleaded.

"Don't do it you moron." Marc urged.

There was a slow build to the organ music as they pushed

aside the cover of the sarcophagus and it came to a thunderous *kaaaaaaaboom.*

Inside was the mummy all wrapped up in bandages except for his black oozing eyes.

"The face of King Hunoptra II. No one has seen him for two thousand years."

"We did in John," said the assistant and she leaned over and gave him a kiss.

Marc and I were grinning. *Oh yeah. This movie is getting somewhere now.*

After they kissed the stupid archaeologist dude blows his moment alone with the girl. He stands there like some doofus and says, "We need to get a crew from the village to help us remove him and the artifacts to the museum."

When they return the mummy is gone. The archaeologist also finds the missing piece from the top of the sarcophagus and translates it. It says—*He who defies the tomb of Hunoptra will unleash an army of the dead.*

The creepy organ music starts in again.

Marc and I look at each other. He makes this creepy mad scientist sound "Whaaaaahaaahaaahaaaa…"

The towns' people cower and mumble amongst themselves and leave the tomb in a hurry.

The archaeologist pulls his assistant close. She is trembling. "There is nothing to fear. It's only an inscription on the tomb to keep away robbers." Then he raises his eyebrows and looks nervously at the ground where giant bandaged footprints lead out of the tomb.

I must have dosed off because the next thing I remember is this scene in the local cemetery. It is dark with a full moon lighting up the old crumbled grave stones and clouds passing in front of the moon. A sinister mist is crawling through the graveyard. There are two guys standing there digging a grave when the organ music picks up again. The next thing you know an army of zombies are walking toward the grave diggers like in that Thriller video. They just stare into space and drool all over the place.

I hear Marc yell, "Get out of there you fools!"

Then the grave diggers see the zombies and start to back up.

Marc says, "What's the matter with your legs you clowns? Run! Run!" Then he turns toward me. "Why are all these fools in these movies such bad runners? It's like they don't know how to even walk. They just stumble around and fall down." Marc turned back toward the TV. "Get up you fool! Get out of there!—too late they got um."

I laughed a little. My stomach was feeling better.

We watched the rest and I guess I dozed off again.

The next thing I remember was hearing the doorbell ring.

Then I dozed off again for a while.

I heard footsteps on the floor above us. They didn't sound normal—kind of like they were dragging their feet.

I smacked Marc in the shoulder. "Wake up dummy!"

He growled at me like a bear awakened too early from hibernation. "Leave me alone."

I walked over to the stairs and listened. There was no talking. But now I could hear three different sets of draggy footsteps moving around up stairs. I started up the steps and stopped when I heard a sedated sort of moan. My heart started to pound out of my chest. I took a couple more steps and looked over the top of the banister. I saw this hunched human walking toward the kitchen. I took a step back down and flattened myself against the wall of the staircase. The step I was on creaked and then the dragging foot sound stopped. It had heard me. I covered my mouth to stop the sound of my heavy breathing. Then the dragging sound began to come toward the stairs. There was a moan from the other corner of the room and a second set of scuffs came toward the top of the steps. I started to back down then a drawn-out face appeared. It looked up from the small device it was carrying, moaned, and then it returned to the device and walked away.

I slipped on the step and fell backward with a loud *thud.* The next thing I remember was looking up at three zombies looking down at me punching in something into the devices they were carrying. My left wrist was all wrapped in bandages. I screamed, "Noooooooo!" and sprang to my feet. "You're not making a zombie out of me!" I flew up the stairs like a rabbit—jumping every three steps, and down the hall to my parents' room. I was screaming like a little girl, "Mom mom!"

She opened the door with another role of bandages. All the blood ran out of my face. I wailed, "Not you too mom! No! No"

The three draggy footsteps made their way down the hallway. I thought to myself. *I'm too young to be part of the undead. How did it come to this?*

My mom scrunched up her face the way she does when she's thinking hard. Then she said, "That's the last time I let you have pepperoni pizza and chocolate before you go to bed. You're lucky you only sprained your wrist the way you're carrying on." Then she mumbled to herself "too much sugar," and walked down the hall past the zombies.

I looked at them a little more carefully. Then a flash of recognition crossed my brain. These were my cousins from Fort Wayne. It had been a few years since I had seen them. I felt like a real doofus making such a fuss. But when we sat down to breakfast and all they did was text people and drool all over themselves I decided I shouldn't be so hard on myself. It was easy to mistake them as zombies. This is definitely one case where my mom is right—too much of that stuff *will* rot your brain. Believe me. I've seen it.

# Hunting at Grandma's house

It was November 15—the first day of hunting season in Michigan. I couldn't wait to get out in the woods. It was my first chance to hunt with a shotgun. All night I had visions of some huge buck coming up to me.

The quiet of the woods gave me a chance to think. Ever since I found out about being adopted I'd been a little edgy and angry. My dad noticed this and told me he was glad they took all the hormones out of the beef and milk. He says things are a lot calmer now. It was making us a race of pumped up angry giants. Dad says if they hadn't taken it out—over time people would have bigger houses, cars, etc.

So far the only person I told about being adopted was Chondra. She hugged me and told me, "Ben—I'll help you find whatever you're looking for. I just want you to be happy." Ever since we were little we could tell each other anything. When I was eight and I stole a candy bar from Bosley's Drug Store. I thought I was going to ____ for stealing. She told me it was OK and I wasn't cursed. She went with me when I confessed to Mr.

Bosley and gave him fifty cents for the candy from my Star Wars piggy bank. He said he was proud of me for being honest. He never told my parents what I did. Still to this day he gives me a wink when we walk in the store.

Buckley was helping me do on-line searches and file fake reports to federal agencies to try to trick someone into providing us protected information. He still thought he was helping me with a research report. His latest idea though had me antsier than a dog on a coon's tale. It involved some pretty serious sneaking and we needed a third person to help us along with a driver. I knew Chondra would be the third person. Marc was a great friend but he couldn't keep a secret. And Wyoming was just too big to hide. The driver would be the hard part. I needed someone on the fringe of society but who was reliable. I asked P.J. Patterson the principal's son. He lived at the other end of our neighborhood in a two story colonial. P.J. got into more trouble than anybody I knew. Plus he was two years older which meant he had a drivers license.

I sat on the base of a downed oak just inside the woods overlooking a fence-line that deer traveled on their way from a big swamp about a mile away. I walked the area every day for the past two weeks checking for tracks, scrapes, and rub lines. I knew this was the perfect spot.

It was about 10:30 now and there was a lot of shooting going on in the area. I heard a series of 6 from Bushley's pot hole. That probably meant they missed. The swamp sounded like World War II. That meant something would be making its' way out of there and come down the fence-line. I watched as three deer came running in my direction. I tucked in behind the roots of the old oak. They were three hundred yards away. The first one was real big. I tried not to breathe knowing they would see my breath in the crisp morning air. I could barely feel my fingers but I took off my gloves to get my hand on the trigger. I started to shake the second I got the gloves off. They were about two hundred yards away now. The lead deer stopped and looked back in the direction they had just come. Then it started to walk down the fence toward me. I still couldn't tell if it was a buck. At a hundred yards I didn't see any antlers. The second deer did have about four point. It was smaller—probably only a year and half, but it was a buck.

I eased the butt of the gun to my right shoulder. I put the crosshairs right on his side. I just had to wait for him to get a little closer. Our area was shot gun only which meant you had to be within a hundred yards to have a decent shot.

A heard a twig snap and turned. About thirty yards directly behind me was a broad beautiful eight point. He was looking directly at me. I didn't dare move or blink. He moved his head from side to side to assess what I was. I thought about turning quickly and taking a shot. A huge fox squirrel jumped across the branches above me. It stopped in the nook of a tree and looked down and laughed at me. I tried to turn slowly toward the eight point. It wasn't slow enough. He jumped and took off through the woods. I hurried to get a bead on him. I took one shot. He didn't flinch and was gone on the other side of the creek that lead to my grandma's house. I turned toward the four point and saw all three of those deer jump the fence and wave their white tails at me as they bound away. The squirrel started laughing again. I looked up and scowled at him. He laughed so hard I thought he was going to fall out of tree.

My walkie talkie screeched and I pulled it out of my orange camo. "Did you get um?" It was my dad on the line. He was setting in a tree stand by the pipeline.

I squeezed the button on the talkie. "No…I missed a nice one."

"Well stay put until noon. I'll meet you back at the shack for lunch."

"OK," I said.

I settled back down in my spot.

A minute later there was a single shot from the direction of grandma's

When I arrived back at the truck to get my hot chocolate for lunch grandma was out in the yard skinning the eight point I saw earlier. She had him hanging in the big maple on the side of the house.

I walked over there. It was a monster—even bigger than he looked in the woods. "Who got him?" I asked.

Grandma was hunched pulling the last of the hide off. "Who you think got um?" She gave me a smirk through her bifocals.

I guessed, "You?"

She turned back to her work. "You and your dad always go way out in the woods and I tell you the best deer always come right across the back yard." She was wiping her knife off on her old jeans. "Some fool out in the woods probably spooked this deer right to me."

"Yeah, some fool," I said.

She started to hose down the inside of the deer. "You see anything this morning."

"Yeah, a couple…Congratulations grandma." I trudged down to the deer shack to meet dad for some soup.

My uncle Ujene was already there. I could hear him snoring when I got to the shack. He was seventy seven and didn't wander far from the camp any more. He mostly came to shoot the breeze and get out of the house. I liked having him there. He told great stories about the one that got away. At least now I could tell one of those stories. I smiled to myself. It was pretty funny that grandma got the buck I spooked. And she shot it right from her back porch.

The rest of hunting season went pretty much the same way. I got a couple more shots but nothing panned out. My uncle said, "There's always next year." He had been hunting for fifty years and only had a few deer but still he kept coming out. There was probably something for me to learn from that.

# Bare skin and Lincolns don't mix

It was mid winter and I was surviving. Hardly anyone even talked about any of my mishaps from the year. A few people like Zonker who's brain had not developed past that of a fish where still harassing me in the halls. I compared his brain to that of a fish because in science class I learned that fish have only a five second memory. That's why when you catch one and toss it back in the water you can catch the same one five seconds later. Zonker is the same way. He tells the same jokes over and over again—unfortunately some of them involve me. I try to ignore him and remind myself that some day he'll be working for me when I get out of college. But it's not much consolation when he's poking at you every time you walk down the hall.

There was one thing that made it easier to survive—that was Buckley. Compared to me Buckley was a total disaster. The first month of school we had swimming in P.E. He emerged from the pool with green boogers hanging from his nose half way down his face. Girls were holding their stomachs like they were going to puke and guys were doubled over trying to catch their breath from laughing so much. He walked around for at least five minutes until Mrs. Sorensen demanded, "What is everyone carrying on for?" Then she noticed the green goop hanging down Buckley's face. "Buckley go in the showers and wipe that gunk off your face."

Everyone burst out laughing. Buckley trudged to the bathroom in his normal gate—shoulders drooping and swimming goggles over his eyes.

It felt good to have people laugh at someone else. It took all the pressure off of me. It also made me feel like a jerk. Buckley was my friend but I let him look like a fool so I wouldn't be the object of ridicule. It made me wonder, *am I turning into the very people I hate? Am I just like everyone else that makes fun of me?*

Unfortunately the answer was yes—and I proved it when we were hit with an early cold spell two weeks before Christmas break.

Our lunch break came. They don't call it recess when you're in high school. That is for little kids. The day of the first good snow, most of the school ate in less than five minutes and went outside for the other twenty five minutes of our "lunch break." It was in the low thirties out but only two or three kids had on coats—Buckley was one of them. The rest of us were "too cool" for that.

There are a few things that don't make sense when you're a teenager—well actually almost nothing makes sense. But if you live in Michigan and you're a teen you don't where a coat because your trying to prove how hip you are or how tough you are. Personally I think it is stupid not to wear something when it is cold enough to freeze water *but* I was out there without one like everyone else.

Buckley was bundled in one of those puffy coats that made

him look like the Pillsbury dough boy. His jacket was so full of feathers that he couldn't even bend his arms. Besides that he was standing behind Wyoming keeping out of the wind. That made Buckley the smartest kid out there—which also made him the target for attacks.

I watched Zonker circle him like some kind of frozen buzzard. He and a couple of his buddies were packing snow balls in their hands and working those fish brains trying to figure out how they could hit Buckley with their frozen fun without hitting Wyoming. Even with the puffy jacket Wyoming was twice as big a target. Finally after circling Buckley for a while they gave up and decided to come my way.

I ran over by Wyoming to "hang out." It was cool having the only freshman to make the varsity football team as your friend.

Still I watched Zonker and his buzzard buddies circle in. He had that duuuuu...huuuu...huuuu...look of his like he was trying to figure something out. I panicked.

"So Buckley, did you ever make your impression on Mr. Handlimper's car?" I asked.

Wyoming turned his back to the wind and faced us.

"What do you mean Ben?" Buckley inquired with this look of innocence.

"Well I know you're from Florida and you wouldn't know about our customs up here." I pointed over to Mr. Handlimper's Lincoln. "But we all have made impressions on his car."

Wyoming crossed his arms with this *what are you up to* look.

Buckley stared over there, "That's the assistant principal's car."

"Don't look at me Buck. I don't make the rules, I just follow them. I thought it was kind of stupid myself. But once you do it you're part of the club." I mustered a look of reassurance.

Buckley had that deep thinking look where he scrunches up

his brow and squints even though he has on those thick heavy rimed glasses that must make him able to see right through a brick wall. Then he started to waddle in his coat toward the car.

Wyoming and I followed him over there. Wyoming still had his arms crossed. He reminded me of a person I saw in a movie that was standing outside of a business. They call um bouncers.

Buckley walked right up to the car. The hood and top were covered with a fresh dusting of snow. The rest was bare metal. He gazed over his shoulders back at the kids in the schoolyard to see if anyone was watching.

No one seemed to be paying any attention. But that was about to change.

Buckley took a deep breath and began to write his name with his finger into the snow on the hood of the car.

Zonker was closing in on us. I could see that the snow ball in his clammy hands had turned into an ice ball. I pulled closer to Mr. Handlimper's car.

"Nice penmanship," observed Wyoming. "You got some nice letters there."

"Thanks," Buckley replied. "Mom says it's important—even if it's a dieing art."

"Well, see you guys later," Wyoming announced. "I'm going inside."

I looked over and saw the gleam in Zonker's eye. I had to think of something fast. "Hay wait a minute Wyoming," I said. "Buckley's not doing the car the *official* way."

He stopped and turned back toward us.

I turned toward Buckley. "You have to make a personalized impression on the car." I wiped out most of his name.

Buckley finished the "r" in Poindexter. "How do I do that?"

I knew if Wyoming heard me he would question it and blow

the whole sceam. I moved over and whispered something in Buckley's ear.

"Are you frickin' serious?"

I'd never heard him swear before. I hesitated a moment. Zonker was tossing his ice from his right hand to his left like it was a baseball and he was about to pitch. It was too much pressure. "Well if you don't want to fit in with the rest of the school that's up to you." I paused. "I was just trying to help you." I pulled back from his ear and mustered my most reassuring smile.

He bought it. He walked over to the Lincoln and looked around to see how many kids were watching. No one seemed to be paying any attention. "No one is watching. How will they know?"

I gave him the fakest *I'm your friend you can trust me* look you've ever seen. "Oh believe me. They'll know."

Buckley looked back at me with a puppy dog trust that sent a dagger through my heart. He then took a deep breath and grabbed the button and zipper on his pants.

I looked over at Wyoming. He had this expression on his face like *what is he doing?*

Then with one big pull Buckley had his pants down to his knees. He bent his backside toward the bare metal on the side of the car.

Three girls screamed when they saw him standing there covering up his front side with his hands.

Everyone turned their eyes toward the screaming girls.

Buckley instinctively backed when the girls pointed at him. Bare butt met bare metal.

The whole courtyard full of eyes followed the imaginary line from the end of the three girls extended fingers.

Buckley grabbed his pants with one hand and covered himself with the other.

Mouths were dropping like dominoes all around the playground. It was too much for Zonker's little fish brain. He dropped the ice ball on the ground and pointed at Buckley. "Haaaa...Haaaa...I see your winky."

Buckley had his pants up to just below his butt. He then tried to pull away from the car but the car pulled back. He tried again and again. "Let me go. You stupid car."

Now the yard irrupted in laughter.

Buckley was pulling but the car was winning. He was glued to the side. He pleaded at me and Wyoming. "Help me guys."

We rushed over there. "Give me your arm," I demanded.

"Give me your other arm," urged Wyoming.

"I can't!" Buckley yelled with his hand trying to hold up his pants and cover his winky at the same time.

Wyoming grabbed his shoulder.

Now people were crowding over by the car trying to get a better look—probably because their views were obstructed by Wyoming.

"On three," demanded Wyoming.

"Don't pull too hard," cried Buckley. "You'll break my arm."

The bell rang but no one went inside.

Mr. Handlimper opened the big double doors that led from the cafeteria to the courtyard. He yelled out, "What are you kids doing by my car."

A bunch of kids turned toward him and took off running inside.

"One...two...*three*," yelled Wyoming. There was a sound like I've never heard before, a blend between paper tearing and the sound of a plunger unclogging a toilet. The car let go of Buckley and he came flying forward.

He was lying face down on top of Wyoming and me with his red irritated butt pointing up to what was left of the crowd.

Mr. Handlimper was almost to the remnants of the crowd that was in scatter mode.

Buckley quickly pulled up his pants, screaming as he hiked them over his flaming red ceaster.

We took off with the last couple of spectators for the double doors. Buckley was moving like he had a bad case of butt sunburn. You could tell every step was a screamer.

Mr. Handlimper was the only one still in the courtyard. He just seemed to be looking around trying to figure out what all the commotion had been about.

He must have found Buckley's heart shaped impression on the car because at the end of the day the PA came on. "Your attention please students." It was Mr. Handlimper. "If anyone knows who made a heart shaped impression with their—a hum—glutious maximus." Everyone laughed in my room except for Zonker who was trying to figure out what a gluta-maxine was. Mr. Handlimper continued, "They should come to my office and turn themselves over—in." We all laughed again. "Thank you and have a good evening."

# Mission impossible

It was Christmas break and time for Buckley's big plan. I was glad he wasn't still mad at me for talking him into putting his butt on Mr. Handlimper's Lincoln—some how it *had* made Buckley more popular—which made me officially the least popular person on the planet.

We met outside of P.J.'s house on December 22. As I already mentioned P.J. was Principle Patterson's son. He got into lots of trouble. So he was perfect for our job. I've noticed that the sons and daughters of principles and ministers get into a lot of trouble. Last summer my friend Bill talked me into going to church camp with him. It might be the fresh air or something but the girls there were crazy. Bill said they acted like sailors who had been at sea for a long time. I'm not sure what he means by that but they *were* crazy. The worst of them was Susie Swanson. She was the daughter of the minister of the church we go to some times. She got caught in several different tents. I guess she has trouble sleeping.

Buckley was already at P.J.'s when I arrived. He said it

would be the perfect time to sneak into the university lab because everyone would be gone for Christmas break.

We piled into the rusty Nissan and took off for Kalamazoo. It was about an hour drive to Western Michigan University. We researched on the web and found out this was the closest place with a DNA isolator.

The university was like a ghost town when we arrived. A few foreign kids were wandering around but all the Americans were gone. P.J. pulled up to the staff only parking place outside the biology research center. I *told you* he was a rebel.

I was starting to get a little nervous. "Are you sure you know how to draw blood." Buckley needed a blood sample to run the analysis.

"Sure," he said reassuringly. "I've seen it done a million times."

"What do you mean *you've seen it done*? You mean this'll be the first time you've done this."

"Sure, but it's perfectly safe—as long as you draw the blood out in one steady motion."

"What happens if you don't?"

He was getting out of the car. "You could get an air bubble in your blood stream and die." He said it matter of fact.

I was thinking to myself, *this is a terrible plan.* But I got out of the car just the same. I had to find out who my parents were. And if this was going to help me find out then it was a chance I had to take.

Chondra, Buckley, and I were on the curb. P.J. was still sitting in the car. I walked over to his door. He looked annoyed but rolled down the window a little. Smoke from his cigarette bellowed out the opening.

"Aren't you coming?" I asked.

He tapped ashes out the window and they landed on my shoe.

"No thanks little dude. I'm staying with my ride." He said it like he was worried someone was gonna steal it. Apparently when he looked at his car he saw only the inner beauty and not the rust and duct tape that the rest of us did. I didn't know it then but in a little while I was going to appreciate his car a lot more.

"OK," I said. Not that I had any choice. I was just hoping he was going to be here when we got out. I wasn't sure if the twenty dollars we gave him was enough to keep him loyal.

The three of us scuttled up to the front doors.

Buckley pulled them, "Looks like they're locked." He turned to C. "What should we do now?"

She put her hands on her hips and glared at him. "What kind of stupid plan is this Buckley?"

He shrugged his shoulders but didn't say anything.

We stood there for a few minutes shivering in the wind.

I could hear the music blaring from the inside of P.J.'s car. I couldn't see inside from all the smoke but I knew that at least it was warm in there.

Then the door to the research center opened from the inside. A wildly haired hunched man with a briefcase burst through and papers showered all over us. "Oh no!" he said. Papers full of numbers and symbols lay in the snow. He kept saying "Oh no! Oh no!"

C started to help him with his papers. Buckley and I dove in. The papers were the same color as the snow so it made it look like the symbols were written right in it.

"Here you go sir." C was handing some to him.

I didn't notice right away but she was stretching to hand them to him. She had one foot holding the door so it wouldn't shut. I smiled to myself glad that I had such a clever friend.

The man jammed the papers in his case. Several were

hanging out when he latched it. He adjusted his taped up glasses and gave us an inquisitive look. "What are you kids doing here?"

I turned to Buckley. This was his plan. I thought he might have something prepared to say. I could see the wheels turning in his head but they weren't getting him anywhere. He had that thinking hard scrunched up look on his face.

C was quicker on her feet. "We came to visit my dad."

The man studied her. I could tell he was about to ask who her dad was. I looked back at C. But she was a mile ahead of me.

"He works in maintenance. He's upgrading the electrical for this building." She pulled open the door. "We're late. He's going to be mad." She nodded for me and Buckley to go inside.

We did as instructed.

"Have a nice day," she said as she pulled the door shut behind her.

I could still see through the little glass window in the door. The man stared at the door for a minute like he wanted to say something. Then he turned and scurried off like a lab rat.

The hall was sterol white and the fluorescent bulb above our heads kept flickering. I was thinking *I hope that isn't a bad omen.*

Buckley finally acted like he knew what he was doing. "The lab is down stairs." He walked down the corridor turned right, left, left, and right. He pushed open the stairwell door.

I tapped him on the shoulder. "Why don't we take the elevator?"

"Sh…" He put his index finger to his lips. "It requires an access card we don't have." He looked past me down the hall like we were in some kind of spy movie or something—then waved us down the stairwell. The lights in there were flickering as well. It made me think about what Buckley told me about science programs being under—funded.

We reached the basement and Buckley pushed open the heavy metal door that said "Restricted."

C grabbed his arm. "Don't they have security cameras or alarms or something?"

Buckley chided her. "This is funded by a grant." He paused for effect. "All grants are a matter of public record. I accessed the file and checked all funding provisions for security." He grinned at Chondra. "There were none—they figure no one would have a reason to break in here." His grin grew. He looked pleased with himself. "They *thought wrong*." His voice was all dramatic.

C shook her head and rolled her eyes. *"Boys"*

I snickered back at Buckley. "Let's git ur done." Mimicking this comedian I heard once.

Buckley then opened the glass doors to a small glassed in room with a bunch of equipment.

There were switches, buttons, knobs, and lots of flashing lights. I hoped he knew how to run this stuff.

He made his way to a well worn office chair. There were more switches in front of it than the cockpit of an airplane. He put in his ear-buds to his i-pod and started playing the theme song to Mission Impossible. It was loud enough for me to hear without the head phones. Then Buckley pulled out some papers he had squished in his back pocket.

I started to get nervous again. "Maybe this isn't such a good idea."

Buckley flipped a series of switches and this thing behind us that looked like some kind of high tech blender started to make noises. The canister thing popped out and made a "poooh" sound followed by what sounded like the noise a bus makes when it pulls up to a stop. He reached in his pocket and pulled out an alcohol wipe and tossed it to C. "Rub down the inside of his arm with this," he yelled. Then he went back to flipping switches.

C rolled up the sleeve on of my sweatshirt.

I just stood there and let her do it. I watched her soft smooth hands carefully rubbed down my arm with the wipe. The alcohol on the wipe made my arm tingle. It must have been pretty strong stuff because as she continued to do it my heart began to race and my whole body started to feel different. I looked into her blue eyes and drifted into them.

Then I heard the sound of paper tearing. I turned as Buckley removed the syringe from it's' package. He slapped my arm a few times with his fingers. Then before I could back out he had the needle in my arm. I thought to myself *whoa that wasn't so bad. I didn't need to get all worked up over this.* I watched as he began to pull bright red blood out of my body into the syringe. I turned to C. Smiled—then everything went black. A minute later I came to. She was holding me up with both arms and Buckley was putting some gauze and a Band-Aid on my arm.

"Nice work Chondra," said Buckley. "You might have saved his life." He took the syringe and shot equal amounts of my blood into three different vials. "When he started to fall the needle almost broke off in his arm."

I started to feel woozy again.

C was still propping me up. "You OK Ben?"

I paused a moment. "Yeah. I'm fine." I started to get up. I didn't want her to think I was some kind of wimp. "I didn't get enough breakfast. Plus it didn't look like lucky Louie here knew what he was doing."

Buckley pulled out his ear-buds. "What did you say?"

"Nothing," I assured him. "What do we do next?"

He sat the three glass vials into little cylinders. There was a mist coming up from the machine.

"What is that thing?" asked C. She leaned up against the glass.

Buckley puffed up his weak chest. "It's a DNA Spectrum Isolator. It analyzes the DNA sequence and breaks down specific inherited traits to determine what characteristics you got from each of your parents." He walked away from the machine. We followed him. "This machine over here can analyze two samples and determine how closely related they are."

I knew Buckley was smart. But I was in awe of his knowledge of all this high tech equipment.

Chondra must have felt the same. "Buckley. How can you know all this?"

He looked like a peacock with its feathers all fanned out. "When I was little my mom worked at NASA. I told you she was a Mission Coordinator on the Space Shuttle—." He stopped himself. "Hey—do you want to do an experiment. Let's take some of my blood and compare it to Ben's for fun. We can find out if we were related a long time ago."

C and I said in unison "Sure!"

Buckley pulled out another syringe.

"Where did you get those anyway?" I asked.

He chuckled at my lack of knowledge, "Medical supply catalogue online." He was rolling up his sleeve and wiping his arm. He opened the syringe and pointed at his arm. Then he stopped.

"What's the matter?" asked C.

"I can't draw the blood from myself. I need both hands."

I had to laugh to myself. At moments Buckley seemed to be

a genius and at others he seemed like the thirteen year old he was.

"What's so funny?" He asked taken back a little.

"Oh nothing," I said.

Then C jumped in. "I'll do it!" She rolled up her sleeve and took the alcohol wipe from Buckley. "Ready!"

Buckley inserted the needle and drew the blood out. I put the Band-Aid over the puncture when he was done.

"Thanks *Ben,*" she said.

There was something about the way she said my name that made me feel different.

Buckley put her blood samples into the analyzer. Then he looked around the lab. "We need to find a protein separating solution. We have to add it to the samples before we run them." He started to delve in drawers.

C and I started to rummage through the lab.

"You didn't finish telling us how you know all this." C was peering in a tall cabinet. "What will the bottle say?"

"It will say PSS .02 parts per million—so my mom was at NASA and she stayed there for the whole time I've been alive. She assisted on planning experiments in space. I went with her to work a lot. They used equipment like this all the time."

I reached into the bottom drawer of the desk. "I found it," I announced.

Buckley added a few drops of the solution to each of our blood samples and turned the machine on.

The DNA analyzer was beeping.

We walked back over to that machine. Buckley pushed a button and a printout came out. He picked up the computer paper. He mumbled to himself, "interesting."

"What! What is it?" I needed to know.

He continued to study the printout.

I was getting impatient. "Come on! Tell me!"

He looked at me. "Your mom had blond hair and blue eyes. Your dad had dark hair and hazel eyes. They are both from European decent." He stopped a moment and mumbled to himself, "that's interesting."

"What!" I was about to explode.

"You will probably turn gray early but you should never go bald."

I was totally irritated. He was reading it like some kind of lab report. Didn't he remember it was about *me*? I stormed out of the room to cool off. Finding out I was going to turn gray early wasn't any help. What was I supposed to do go to Florida and wander around asking people if their ancestors were from Europe and check if they had grey hair? Didn't he know how many people had gray hair in Florida?

C came out in the hall. "Come on Ben. I know this is frustrating but Buckley's doing his best to help."

I knew she was right.

We went back in the lab.

Buckley was in front of the other machine. "I've found something else interesting. You two are not even remotely related and your blood types are compatible for marriage.

Our eyes met for a second. I blushed a little.

We made our way back to the desk where Buckley was studying the reports. He kept saying, "hmmmmmm." Then he would fiddle with his glasses and rub his chin. He did this several times and each time he would look over his shoulder at me.

I started to get irritated again. "What is it Buckley!"

He sat the paper down, took off his glasses, and stood right in front of me. There was an inquisitive look on his face. "Chondra do you think you can help me draw some blood from myself."

"Sure. Why?"

"There's just something that I'm curious about." He sat back at the desk wiped off his arm with another swab and prepared a syringe.

"How many of those things did you bring?" It seemed to me that he only needed the one for my test.

He was chuckling at the question. "It's actually cheaper if you buy a bunch of them. It cost $10 for a hundred or $12 for a dozen. Obviously—I bought a hundred."

He inserted the needle in his arm. "I can hold it steady. You just need to draw it out in one steady motion." He was nodding encouragement at C.

She put her steady hands on the syringe and in a few seconds it was full.

"Nice work." Buckley was complimentary. "You'd be a great pilot or doctor."

"Thanks Buck. That's very sweat."

He had a big toothy grin for a moment. Then he went to splitting the samples and running them through the two DNA machines.

We waited for a few minutes while the big blender did it's thing with his blood samples. It made that loud bus like air brake sound again which meant the test was done.

Then we heard another sound. It was the sound of the glass door slamming behind us.

We turned and saw an overweight resentful night guard standing behind us.

I peered at his badge. It said "Special Officer Wimpley." If I wasn't so scared I might have laughed at a security guard named Wimpley. I bet when he was training to be a guard he probably got harassed a lot and called names like Wimpy Wimpley or Wimpo Wimpley, or the Wimpmiester.

I could tell by the scowl on his face that he wanted to take some latent rage out on a few trespassing kids. "What are you doing here?"

We could tell that this wasn't really a question. We translated his words—"When I get a hold of you you're dead."

He started to back us into a corner. There was an evil grin on his face as he tapped his night stick against the equipment.

Buckley said, "I wouldn't do that sir...that's expensive equipment."

At this remark the guard's eyes seemed to turn red. Maybe it was a reflection from all the blinking lights but it scared me to death.

We scattered like lab rats in every direction. Buckley dove under a table and out the other side. C leaped across the table top like a hurdler and was the first one out the door.

I tried to take the direct rout but felt a tug. He had the tail of my shirt. I swung my arm at him but couldn't get loose.

Buckley was now out the door and heading down the hall for the stairs.

"You're not getting away from me kid." I could sense the glee in his voice. This was probably his first bust ever in twenty years.

I swung at his hands in desperation but they were too strong. I was doomed. I stopped struggling. "You got me sir. I wasn't doing anything—*honest*. I was looking for my mom." I stood still and heard a jingling sound. I looked backward and he was pulling his handcuffs from his utility belt. They weren't coming loose easy. I knew he had to let go of my shirt for a second to get it unhooked from the belt.

"Don't *you* move," he said. Then he let go of me.

I waited until he took his eyes off me to try to figure out how the handcuffs came off his belt. He looked down. Then I took off with more adrenalin than I had ever felt in my body. In seconds I was out the door and up the stairs. I could hear his footsteps right behind me echoing up the stairwell. My heart was a base drum.

I reached the top and hesitated for a moment. *Did we come right then left or left then right? And if we go back then it would be the opposite.* Then I felt a hand grab my shoulder. *Oh know. He caught me again* I thought. It pulled me down the hall to the right. I realized it was C.

Buckley was yelling down the corridors. "This way! Hurry!"

C and I ran toward him as hard as we could. Wimpley was almost on top of us. I could smell his Dr. Pepper and Cheeto breath on the back of my neck.

We turned the corner and headed toward the outside door. He lost a few steps on us at the corner so we had a slight lead on him now.

Buckley was yelling out the door to P.J. "start the car!!!"

Then I saw him dash out the door.

C and I were panting like crazy—but not as bad as Officer Wimpley. He was wheezing and gasping for air like a chain smoker.

C and I burst through the door. I slipped a moment and fell on the icy sidewalk. My butt hurt like crazy from the fall but I was too pumped up to worry about it so I jumped up and dove into the car. I yelled. "Go! Go! Go!"

P.J. flicked his cigarette out the window. "Stop the yelling you goof balls. What's with all the drama?"

Then Wimpley burst through the door. He glared down at us sitting in the car, and bent over for a second to catch his breath.

P.J. turned to Buckley. "What did you kids do?"

Buckley didn't know what to say.

C reached over the back seat and grabbed P.J.'s collar.

"Unless you want to be arrested as an accessory and have your dad pick you up in jail you better get this bucket of bolts moving *now!*"

His eyes bulged open at the thought of being busted. He quickly turned the ignition. The car tried to start but wouldn't. It just kept making this pathetic clicking noise.

Wimpley was now half way to the car. He pulled out his radio and was talking to somebody.

P.J. tried the key again—nothing.

We could hear a siren somewhere in the distance.

C yelled, "get this thing moving!"

"I'm trying!" P.J. started talking to his car. "Come on baby. Let's go. Daddy loves you."

C was shaking her head.

Then we heard the car leap to life.

Wimpley was by the hood.

P.J. nervously shifted into reverse and slammed on the pedal. We lurched backward across the lot and over a curb.

Then P.J. put it in drive and floored it. The engine roared but we didn't move.

"What's the matter now!" C's voice was urgent and irritated.

P.J. looked out his side view mirrors. The back tires were hanging in the air off the curb. "Somebody's got to get out and push."

C and I looked at each other. Without a word we were out the back doors pushing on the rear bumper. "Try it again," we yelled in unison.

The siren was getting closer.

P.J. was all business now. The thought of being busted had sharpened his normally dull senses. He shifted it to first gear and gave it some gas.

Wimpley was crossing the lot with his talkie in his hand. "We got um now Charlie." His face was full of Christmas morning glee even though it was a few days away.

I didn't want to be his early present so I pushed with all my might.

The car lurched forward and I fell face down in the snow. As I raised my head I was met by pieces of pavement and snow being thrown in my face by the peeling tires.

C helped me to my feet and we chased after the car.

P.J. stopped for just a moment and we dove into the back seat like the cops were shooting at us.

We all slipped and swerved ourselves out of there in P.J.'s rusty Nissan. C and I were lying sprawled across the back seat. We looked at each other and started to laugh harder than I ever remember laughing. Buckley and P.J. joined in as we made our way back home. I didn't learn much about my mother and father but I did learn something about Buckley and C on our trip. They were the best friends in the world.

# The one and only time I stayed at Steve's house

Winter was dragging along and I kept mulling over books and stuff on the web. My mom must have thought that was unhealthy so she set up for me to go to an old friend's house. Steve and I had been friends since we were in Cub Scouts. We never did earn many badges, but we did like playing outside. I guess we really bonded when we were in the Pine Wood Derby. If you don't know what that is—it is where you spend a couple weeks making little wooden cars and then you race them down this ramp. The project is designed to give boys an opportunity to build something with their father and learn about engineering and aerodynamics and stuff like that. I ended up learning a couple of different lessons. See—my dad and I worked real hard and made this sweet looking car. We followed every rule for the contest. When it was the big day of the race I was pacing around and couldn't *wait* until our race started. My dad and I were smiling—it was one of those real father son moments. The head of scouting stepped up and called out our name and *Tom Wilkinsin's*. He was the *Mayor's* son.

We placed our cars at the top of the ramp. I felt the smooth finish of my car. Dad and I used ten different grits of sandpaper until it was as smooth as a baby's bottom. It was one fine looking racer.

The scout leader said, "Ready…set…go!"

I looked on in anticipation.

The ramp angled down at about thirty degree for the first thirty feet. Then it flattened out until you crossed the finish line.

My car took off flawless. There was not a single wobble in any of the wheels. I smiled as it glided down the ramp effortlessly. Smooth as silk. My machine was at one with the universe—an example of perfection in the making.

Then I glanced over at *Tom's* car. My eyes flickered and my head convulsed from the shock. It was like I had just been blasted with a stun gun. *Tom's* car was already across the finish line and he and his dad were smiling for the photographer from the Daily News. My car was still traveling down the ramp.

A sea of scouts stampeded over me to congratulate Tom and to get their picture in the paper. It was like a guppy trying to swim up stream as I made my way to my car and my dad. When I got to him he smiled and said, "Nice work son. I'm proud of you. You made one fine car there."

Then he put his hand up to his chin—like he does when he is thinking real hard. When we got home my dad made a call to the regional head of the scouts. He told me to go out and play, but I listened in from outside the kitchen window. This is what I heard.

Dad: "I don't have any proof but it just seems like something is fishy."

Other man: "?????????????????"

Dad: "It seems like if it was done honestly they would have nothing to hide."

Other man: "????????????????"
Dad: "I know who he is—but scouts are not about that."
Other man: "?????????????'
Dad: "I'd appreciate that. Thank you so much for your assistance. You have a good day too."

When I heard dad hang up I scurried over by the garage and started pitching my rubber baseball against the side. I always like playing there. When no one was around I would play imaginary baseball games there. I would pitch the ball and then field it and tag out the guy on first. Those were some real intense games. It's not easy playing every position.

It was a couple of weeks later that I found out what happened. After the phone call the regional coordinator paid a visit to the Wilkinson's. When he inspected Tom's Derby car they found the front end was loaded down with lead weights that were hidden inside. Tom was disqualified from participating in the state meet. But since his dad was friends with the reporter that came out for the original photos, no one came to do a story about their cheating. I guess when a paper makes someone a hero they don't want to make themselves look stupid. So the two things I learned from the Pine Wood Derby and from scouts were "Don't trust a politician" and "If it seems too good to be true it probably is."

Sorry about that. I was starting to tell you about my friend Steve. He lived out by Gun Lake. My mom liked their family so she kept in touch with his mom. Well one thing led to another and I was invited to Steve's to stay a night. I think my mom thought it would be good for me to get out of the house.

It was late in the winter and according to the weather women on local T.V. it was a roller coaster ride—you know, up and down.

Steve was standing on the porch with a goalie helmet, pads,

and a stick when I arrived. He handed them to me and said, "Let's go. The big A's are waiting on us."

*Oh great*, I thought to myself. *I'm going to die.* I just didn't know how close I was to being right.

We arrived at the ice about twenty minutes later. I was exhausted. *You* try and walk a mile and a half in goalie gear. After I wiped the stinging sweat out of my eyes, I was surprised to see a perfectly made rectangular rink. This should have been my first warning. Natural lakes don't form in perfect rectangles. Or maybe it should have been the ten foot high fence with barbed wire at the top that we snuck under to get in. But when you're a teenage boy it's like those things are invisible—I mean you really don't see them!

Steve was really serious about his ice skating. There had to be twenty guys there. He even had a dude be the announcer and ref. Most of them I didn't know. Gun Lake was at the cross roads of four different school districts so I figured that explained it. Plus Steve—being as serious as he was about the ice—probably found every guy in the county who could skate. As I watched some of the guys warm up I deduced why he was going to put me in at goalie—these guys were ten times better than me. I would never be able to keep up with them on the ice.

His strategy to use me was this: "Ben—squat down like this in front of the goal. If you think somebody is going to shoot fall down on the ice in front of the net like this." He dropped down on the ice. So I understood my role. I was a speed bump in front of the goal.

The game started out OK. Well, if you were on the other team. This blond haired kid that everybody nicknamed Greatzky smoked me two times in the first five minutes. I dropped down on the ice and he shot right over me.

Then the big event happened.

\*\*\*

Some guys' little sister showed up with a stick and skates and dashed out onto the ice and slipped right in front of me.

The announcer dude blew a whistle and yelled, "Stop the game!" The players all began to stop where they were. Big-A-One turned to look at the announcer as he was skating backwards and then turned to stop—too late. As he spun around he saw that a young girl lay on the ice in front of him. It was simply not enough time, his momentum carried him forward and he crashed right on top of her.

The other players rushed over and circled around the young girl who was lying under Big-A-One. If you haven't perceived the seriousness of the situation yet it is because you don't know the "Big A's." The "Big" part was because they were so *big*. The "A" part of their names was because a certain part of their bodies were *so big*. The "One" and "Two" came from the fact they were twin brothers and were born a few minutes apart.

"Hey! Big-A-One! Get off that girl! You're going to smother her!" yelled one of the boys.

I slipped and slidded my way into the circle.

Greatski made his way into the crowd of boys. "Help me get A-One off that poor girl." Three boys jumped in helping him pull Big-A-One back to his feet, which was no easy task. It was simple physics. A body in motion stays in motion, until acted upon by an outside force. And when the body in motion is Big-A-One then whatever it hits is going to feel it. Once Big-A-One was on his feet again he looked at Greatski and in a not so astute sounding voice said, "Sorry!"

Greatski knelt beside the young girl who lay unconscious on the ice.

"Uhh…is she OK?" asked Big-A-One in his rather slow but concerned way.

I knelt down and put my head on her heart. "She's breathing."

A sigh of relief came from Big-A-One, and then from the rest of the boys. Everyone knew that Big-A-One was capable of smothering a person to death. Most of the boys had been crushed by him one time or another and had barely escaped with their lives.

"I don't think we should move her. She could have some broken bones," suggested Steve.

Just then there was a cracking sound that sent chills through every ones mind.

"Big-A's get off the ice," yelled Greatski.

The ice continued to split and crack. Boys began racing off the ice in all direction like the ripples caused by tossing something in a pond. The Big-A's started backing away from the center of the ice, looking nervously in all directions as cracks began to form around their feet and up and down the whole rink.

"We have to move her. *Now*!!!" said Greatski, as he picked up her head

and shoulders and Steve grabbed her legs. A crack formed between them as they carried her off. "Run! Now!" yelled Greatski as the crack widened. The crack now almost engulfed the two boys as they jumped to safety.

Just as they reached shore I looked around. I was the only one still on the ice. I stood but slipped. The pond groaned and released an awful stench. It was worse than the Wimpley's breath.

I stood to take another step—looked over to the shore—smiled—and fell through the ice.

I surfaced for a second among little brown logs that floated around my head. I coughed out some smelly yellow liquid, grabbed the edge of the ice and slipped under once more.

"He's fallen through!" announced a boy standing by the side of the rink. "Somebody help!" yelled another.

I was in the icy water grabbing for the edge of the hole. As I tried to grab the edge of the hole, it continued to break. A current of water was pulling me under. For some reason my mind flashed to when I was a little kid. I could see my mom talking to me. "Don't go in too deep honey. The Under Toad will get you." Right there in the pond of filth as I was being pulled further and further down I swear I saw the Under Toad crouched down on the murky bottom, with red beady eyes and a sinister grin. I began to panic. It was too much for me to fight against.

"Grab the rope! Chain gang!" ordered Greatski as he raced across the ice avoiding the cracks. The other boys instantly followed him without hesitation. He dove down on the ice and slid half way into the hole, reaching down his arms into the icy water and catching my panicking arms as I slipped into the dark depths. Steve grabbed his legs. Then two arms grabbed Steve's legs, and so on, until a chain of boys laid flat across the ice. A rope was quickly tossed out and one by one the boys were pulled off the ice, along with me, who couldn't wait to get back on dry land. Steve and Greatski were shaking and their teeth were chattering.

Steve looked over at me and said, "Oh'—"

"—Crap!" Greatski finished.

That was the end of the hockey game. Everybody dispersed like I was some kind of leper or something.

Steve and I were the only ones left.

He looked at me and groaned, "man—nobody will want to wear *that* again."

I yelled back, "What!"

"Nobody's goin' to want to wear that stuff!"

I shook my head to the side to get the water out of it—but it wasn't water that was in there.

We started to make our long trek back to his house. We were shivering so bad we looked like two off balance washing machines shaking down the road.

I must have been a funny sight because Steve started laughing like a frozen chipmunk. I scowled at him—then chattered along. I was thinking to myself, *I'm glad there isn't much traffic around. We must look like a site.*

When we finally arrived at his house his mom greeted us at the door. "You two aren't coming in *my* house."

"We're f…f…freezing m…m…mom."

"Then you better get that stuff off quick. I'll get the hose out of the shed. You hurry up."

We stood there—pillars of determination and strength, vowing not to give in. If you're a freshman boy you don't take your clothes off in front of your mom or any girl—especially if you're frozen solid. There's only one exception to this long standing rule. If you're covered in human excrement and it's in your ears and up your nose, and you believe it's possible your friends' mom will leave you in the yard as a statue until spring.

So we commenced to stripping on the spot. Steve's mom was blasting us with the hose and we were pulling and tugging off the poopy stuff. It really wasn't a big deal until we got down to our underwear.

Steve's mom turned off the nozzle for a second. "All of it boys—that stuff isn't coming into *my* house. I should toss it straight into the fire pit."

Then it got tricky. It's not that easy to take your underpants off when you're frozen, being blasted by water, and trying to cover up your privates. As cold as it was though we didn't need both hands to cover ourselves up. Once we had everything off as luck would have it Steve's senior sister Sarah walked out onto the porch. "What's that awful smell?" she inquired. Then she saw us in our frozen state and broke down laughing. She was standing there pointing at us with one hand and holding her side to keep her guts from falling out from all the laughter. If Guinness Book was there she would have broken the world record for "not breathing for the longest period of time." Her face was beat red and I swear she didn't take a breath for almost five minutes she was laughing so hard.

Our luck continued as the traffic picked up and people were slowing down to see what they couldn't believe. When your driving along heading to where ever it is that you're going, the last thing you expect to see are two skinny white naked butts on the side of the road.

Steve's sister yelled, "wait right there I want to get a picture of this for my Face Book. This is too funny." She dashed off.

Steve held up his hand to stop the onslaught of water and looked at his mom with pleading puppy dog eyes. "Mom! For God' s sake let us get dressed."

She shut the hose off and tossed us a couple of towels—just seconds before Sarah came out with the camera. "Oh' drat! I'm too late."

Steve stuck his blue tongue out at her.

She clicked a quick shot and grinned. "This will still be worth something someday for blackmail."

Steve chased after her, "Give me that you rat!"

After our showers and some dry clothes we were ready to

play some more. We ended up in Steve's tree house—actually
it was a stilt house that leaned against a tree. It had three ten foot
4 x 4's as legs and the tree was the fourth leg. It was pretty cool.
It had a roof and all the walls were finished with a hodge-podge
of material. There was drywall, old boards, new boards, metal
sheeting, and plastic. In the small holes and cracks he had
jammed in old baseball card, corn cobs, sneakers, and dog chew
toys—anything to keep out the draft.

When I climbed inside the fort made noises like it wasn't
happy we were there.

I studied all the things in there. Steve had old blankets, along
with binoculars, stale snacks, pathetic pillows, besieged board
games, an etch a sketch with only one working knob, and a
couple of well worn hand held games from the dark ages—
everything a boy needs to survive in the wild.

I noticed a cool comic crammed in a crack along one of the
walls. I pulled it out from where it was wedged and leaned
against a wall to have a look.

The next thing I remember is Steve looking down at me, his
sister snapping pictures with her cell phone, and his mom lifting
my eye lids and saying, "are you ok?" As crazy as it sounds the
only thing I could think of was *I'm glad it's not those two med
techs looking down at me again.*

# Easter eggs and auditoriums full of people don't mix

There are two places that its' likely you wont find a freshman boy. One of them is in the Varsity locker room—well unless you like swimming in downward swirling water with large brown objects hitting you in the head each time they come around. The second is at a tryout for a theatre production of some musical. But if you happen to know that Buckley's mom *loves* the theatre and that she insists that he be exposed to this *wonderful* opportunity. Then it's likely you might find a bunch of freshman boys risking certain embarrassment and permanent scaring of their self image on the stage.

This year's production was Okalahoma—complete with tumbleweed, bushes, and real farm animals. Theatre just wasn't cool for boys to be in at our school. So the lead parts ended up going to Alabama Jackson—the only kid in our school with a southern accent—being from Mississippi. The lead girls' part went to Danielle Armstrong—she sung like an angel and looked right at home tending to the animals. The next important girls' part went to my friend Chondra. She played Odo, a rather energetic and frolicking young lass. I always saw her in shorts and jeans. She played ball with use, made forts, and talked trash as well as the rest. It was a real eye opener seeing her in a dress. I got the part of Will—Ode's fiancé who she chases around the whole play. I didn't realize how realistic this play was or the irony in it until much later.

Rehearsals went well for the most part. Wyoming played Haus a huge field hand with very few lines. His costume required special attention from the volunteer seamstress. No one knows for sure but rumor is she stitched together three old costumes to make his. It did look rather eclectic.

Marc played the skinny wise cracking field hand "Marc." I know what you're thinking, *there's no character named "Marc" in Oklahoma.* Well—there was in our production. During tryouts Marc was winging the part he hadn't rehearsed for. It was like watching a night at the Improves. He had Miss Dubose rolling in the isle—really, she started at the back of the theatre and rolled all the way down to the stage. Buckley got it on camera and we posted it on You-Tube. We have almost ten thousands hits. Don't worry, teachers never check out Y.T. so we're safe. Well, after that she had an assistant collaborate with Marc to write his own lines. Buckley played a bumbling cook. He spilled a lot of slop and banged pots together. His mom was so proud.

On the night of the big début we were fluttering around back stage like a flock of geese in a cage. The girls were in one dressing room and us boys were in the other.

Wyoming was sweating bullets. It looked like somebody turned on a faucet over his head and left it on. He had to be sweating off a pound a minute. I laughed to myself thinking, *if I signed up Wyoming for that T.V. show The Biggest Loser, and then had him weigh in after our performance—he would win for sure.* At the rate he was sweating pretty soon there would be nothing left of him.

He paced back and forth over by the Cows practicing his three lines. "Whoa girl," "That's a nice hat maam," and "You' all go' in down to dat barn dance."

I peeked out through the curtains. The auditorium was filling to the rafters. People were climbing over top of each other, standing in the isle, and sittin on laps.

Ms. Dubose yelled "places everyone!"

I swallowed hard and I moved over to my spot on the set. The first scene took place on the front porch of the farm house. It was at that moment that I realized that stage fright was a real medical condition. I had memorized all my lines in one night— but now I couldn't remember a single one. I started breathing harder.

I sat down on the steps of the porch.

The curtain opened.

The crowd hushed.

A big spotlight pierced the dimness and lit up the stage.

Buckley walked into the scene carrying a bucket of milk that sloshed from side to side spilling out onto the floor and all over his legs.

You might be thinking O' Oh', but he was supposed to do that. But that was the end of things going the way they were supposed to.

Buckley sat the bucket on top of the fence post next to the corral. We all watched in anticipation. He had spilled the bucket every time during practice. He moved his hands and let go of it. It stayed there perfect. He looked over at us and grinned. His mom was so proud. All of us on the porch sighed with relief.

Marc said, "Jumpin Jiminy! You got any cookies to go with

that Buckley?" Of course you know those weren't his real lines. The audience laughed at Marc's response and we did too.

I don't know if it was the release of anxiety from the laughing but I felt all the muscles in my body let loose for a second. Then a terrible thought ran across my mind. *Why did I take that bet and eat a dozen Easter eggs.*

The auditorium was filled with cheers and laughter.

It took a few seconds and then I got up from the front porch.

The rest of the cast was looking at me because I wasn't supposed to get up yet.

C, who had been sitting next to me on the porch scrunched up her face and looked over at the farm animals.

It hit Buckley next. He got this look of intense pain on his face and backed away. It was at this point that luck would have it Buckley backed into the fencepost and knocked over the milk bucket on top of his head. The pig and cow came over and started giving Buck a tongue bath slurping up the milk. They bumped the fence—and being a set it began to tumble like a bunch of dominoes. One section after another, then the last of the fence fell against the cow causing it to back up letting out an audible blast of flagilence.

But the real smell was making its' way out from the source of the explosion. It was like Mr. Openhiemer was down in my stomach working with all those Easter eggs I ate to make a new kind of bomb. I couldn't help myself another blast came out. This time I heard it. But pandemonium was breaking out on the stage and no one else did. I quickly started to back away from myself—which was a big mistake. You can't lose yourself even if you are trying. The smell was a living force, an entity in itself. It was alive! And the more I moved away from the places I had been the more I was spreading it around.

The audience now was doubled over in laughter. This was

the funniest play any of them had ever seen. I looked over at miss Dubose. Her face was contorting as if it was made with Silly Putty. You know if you press it against a picture in a newspaper you can stretch it all sorts of strange ways. I figured it was the smell but since she was in the back of the audience I ruled that out.

Marc came stumbling over to me then dropped to the floor like he was trying to escape the smoke of a burning building— he really is a pretty good actor. Chondra was crying and rubbing her eyes which were the color of a chili pepper. Buckley was trying o give himself the Heimlich over a fence rail.

Then it hit the audience like an invisible green tidal wave. Panic and chaos took over. A man in the back of the auditorium stumbled to his feet and pulled the fire alarm. In one huge mass the crowd pushed it's way to the exits.

Marc jumped off the stage and looked up at me. He had his shirt pulled up over his mouth. "Get outa' there Ben!" There was a look of panic in his eyes.

I felt like Wyoming must have felt when the whole Caledonia team was chasing after him. Except the only thing chasing me was coming from inside of me. The gas was clawing it's way out like an angry Jeanie that had been trapped in a lamp for a thousand years. I dove off the stage the way those people do at big concerts. "Help me! Help me!"

C gave me this "You really are good at acting look."

The people I was body surfing on dropped me.

One guy was rubbing his eyes in pain saying, "make it stop."

Two little girls were crying for there mom.

I caught a glimpse of the fire chief. He was telling every one to "remain calm." But he was pushing his way to the exit like everyone else.

I determined one thing. When it comes to a real life and death situation like this—all that training we do for emergencies gets thrown out the window, which is where I wished I was.

When I got outside the air never smelled so fresh. I found Marc in the mayhem he said, "I never knew a cow fart could be *so* bad." He was taking deep breaths.

I quickly decided to support his theory that the cow caused the chaos to cover up any more embarrassment for myself. So I started walking around the crowd planting a little subliminal message in everyone's brain. "Man that cow stunk!" And I didn't have to feel guilty about doing it. I figured I might have saved its life. I mean who would even consider eating a cow that smelled that bad?

# Spring is in the air

It was starting to get warm. Well that's what we call it in Michigan. It was around fifty during the day and the sun was out a lot. I've noticed that people really get into spring and summer a lot more in the north. When you're all cooped up like a bear in a cave all winter and the weather turns nice everyone goes buzerk. Their adrenaline is pumping out of control and they run around everywhere screaming.

There were birds singing and building nest and little baby rabbits were hopping around our yard eating my mom's flower shoots.

But this spring was a little different. I was antsyier than normal. I think maybe there was more oxygen in the air or something. I asked Buckley if that was possible. He scrunched up his face like he does every time he's thinking hard. Then he offered a spocke-ish explanation "It's logical that there might be more oxygen since all the plant life is starting to grow. But I've never actually read a study. Maybe we should get a grant and scrutinize the anomaly."

# REGINALD RAAB

I only had two things on my mind. Finding out who my real mom was—and of course girls. Anomalies with oxygen would have to wait. Chrissie Allen had decided after the "bee incident" that we would be better off as friends. She talked to me at school but I could see our romantic spark was gone. I think when she saw me now she couldn't get out of her mind the hideous creature she went to the movies with. And McKayla wouldn't give me the time of day since I was at the bottom of the food chain and she was at the top. I do find it ironic that the most affluent of human beings that are at the apex of the food chain covet the lowest forms of existence as the most valuable. For example the wealthiest people in the world eat snails and fish eggs and have algae drinks. You don't see any of them eating other people. Clearly we're not as valuable as we think.

Anyway I spent most of my time researching Genetics with Buckley and Chondra and trying to tap into secure networks in Cook County Florida where my parents adopted me.

Buckley came up with a plan to get us down there. The trick was to get our parents to let us go. After all—we were only freshman and Buckley technically was only a seventh grader in age.

After several weeks of putting on a charade of responsibility: volunteering to take out trash, wash dishes, do laundry, and use our manners at the table, our parents had talked together and agreed it was OK for us to go stay with Buckley's Uncle Jimmy in Orlando for spring break.

When we exited the airport the only thing there to greet us was a blast of oppressive jungle air. The air was so heavy it felt like somebody was sitting on my chest. Buckley was down on the pavement rummaging through his carry-on bag.

Chondra looked down at his spindly frame. "What you lookin for Buck?"

He pulled out a hand full of inhalers and started shaking them one at a time. When he found one to his satisfaction he dropped the others and sucked in a big blast of albuteral.

"You all right?" I asked.

He stood back up and answered in a wheezy breathed shroud. "Yeah...just needed my kryptonite."

There was a honk and a hazy holler from down terminal D where we were waiting. *This must be Uncle Jimmy* I thought.

He was standing there in a flower print shirt and waving at us. "Over here Buckley!"

We grabbed the bags and fought our way down the sidewalk. It brought back a funny memory of Marc telling about taking his sister to the airport. But it also seemed like a metaphor on my life. I always seemed to be walking against traffic.

Chondra whacked me in the side with her bag and whispered to me. "I thought only tourist wore those kind of shirts."

I chuckled as we reached the trunk of his big white Lincoln.

"Well—you must be Ben and Chondra." He gave us a big toothy grin which let me know he was Buckley's relative and helped toss our luggage in the trunk. Then he gave Buckley a hug. "Good to see you boy."

Buckley took shot-gun and C and I climbed in the back. The frozen vinyl crunched as we sat down. The air conditioning was blowing so hard I thought I was in a blizzard.

C reached in her pocket and pulled out a rubber band to put her hair up out of her face. It made her look older and exposed her long lean neck.

I rubbed my hands together to warm them as Jimmy made small talk with Buckley about his school year and the new house up in Michigan. When Uncle Jimmy said, "I can't live up there it's *too cold*." I started snickering.

Chondra punched me in the side as if to say "straighten up," but she was laughing under her breath.

Jimmy inquired in the rear view mirror. "You kids alright back there?"

"Sure," we answered in stereo.

"Is this your first time to Florida?"

"Yes sir," responded Chondra. "But Ben was born here."

Buckley was staring out at the palm lined boulevards and yards with pink plastic flamingoes. "Yeah…we came to find out—."

Chondra interrupted him. "What Disney World looks like…" She paused a second coming up with more to say. "Ben was so small when they moved to Michigan…and I've never been down here."

Buckley slumped in his seat even further than usual. I could tell he realized he almost gave away our plan.

We didn't say much more the rest of the drive to Jimmy's. For some reason a picture of Buckley in one of those interrogation rooms with the two way mirror was planted in my brain. A Detective was about to ask him some questions and he started spattering out everything he knew.

We pulled in Uncle Jimmy's garage and he shut the door remotely before we even got out. When I opened the car door I was shocked to find that his garage was even air conditioned.

Inside was even colder. I expected to see penguins waddling around. I worried that I hadn't brought the right kind of clothes to stay there for five days.

He showed us to our rooms. C got a small room that I guessed Jimmy used for exercising. It had a tred-mill and one of those exercise bikes and an air mattress on the floor.

"You work out a lot Mr. Manten sir?" Chondra was making small talk.

"Call me Jimmy." He stretched his arms above his head. His Hawaiian shirt pulled up over his loping belly. "Yep...pretty regular. This body is a well oiled machine."

I looked down at the odometer on the bike. It showed 1.3 miles. "How long you had this Uncle Jimmy?" I inquired.

"About ten years." He started bending his knees doing calisthenics. When he got to the bottom of his squat and belched he reminded me of a bullfrog. "Let me show you boys to your room. Then we can have some lunch." He started to give us advice. "You can't spend all your time exercising. Part of training is making sure you eat plenty of protein to build strong muscles."

I was pretty sure he was good at the second part of his training.

He let Buck and I settle into his only spare bedroom. There was a set of Teenage Mutant Ninja Turtle bunk beds in there.

I took the top because I figured it might be warmer up there. "Why's your uncle got these?"

Buckley was closing the air conditioning vents for our room. "He's divorced. But his two boys stay with him every other weekend and on holidays." He opened his bag and put on a sweatshirt.

I opened mine and donned a long sleeve t-shirt—the warmest thing I had. "Why didn't you tell me this place was so cold?"

"I kind of forgot."

"Then how did you know to bring a sweatshirt?"

He looked at me matter-of-factly. "My mom packed my bag—come on let's get some lunch."

I followed him out the door and murmured to myself. "I hope

it's a hot lunch." I pictured myself coming back from spring break with frost bite.

In the kitchen there were three plates of food setting out for us. I understood more about Jimmy's training diet. On the counter there were take-out boxes from every restaurant in Orlando. And on our plates were different kinds of Chinese food, slices of pizza, and peanut butter sandwiches. I was guessing this was the only thing he knew how to make.

We sat down in the bar stools at the counter.

I started on the pizza. It looked the safest. "What does your uncle do?"

Buckley was using his fork like a backhoe and vacuuming up some Moo Goo Guy Pan. "He's a…" he paused to finish slurping, "Chef."

I gazed out the glass sliders that led out to the back yard. Jimmy was cleaning the pool with one of those nets on an extension pole. I was thinking to myself *I'm glad my dad sold his restaurant or he might have turned out like him.* It also made me start to think about finding my mom. "When are we gonna try to sneak into the County records office."

Buckley had his head in the fridge scouring for refreshment. "You guys want a Coke or milk."

C was staring out the slider at Uncle Jimmy taking off his shirt. "I think I'll have some milk to settle my stomach."

"I'll take a Coke," I said.

Buckley stood at the other side of the counter looking out at us. "I think we should start with the adoption agency. The security should be slacker."

C gave Buckley a hard look like a bull that sees red. "*That's* what you *said* about the university and we almost got *busted* by officer *want-to-be* Wimpley."

Buckley backed away from the counter and took a big sip of his milk—leaving a white stash over his upper lip.

Once again the thought—*I'm trusting this guy. He's the brains of the outfit* sprang to life in my head. I knew I had to be desperate to follow him into another secure area. But the fact of it is *I was!* So I backed him up. "Come on C you know we went over the plan several times. Those agencies don't expect anyone to sneak in there. So we hang out the first day and take turns sitting in the lobby and watching from the front door for when people take their lunch and lock the place up."

Buckley felt a little more confident with my support. "Yeah that's right...and *I* have my mom's video camera to record when people leave and the layout of the building."

C stood up from her stool and made her way to scrape the leftovers into the waste basket. "Are you still gonna do that stupid idea of carrying around a clip board and asking questions for some school report?"

"Hay—I thought that was a pretty good idea. Buck found a school near here that is not on break this week and even got the name of the journalism teachers to use for our cover. I thought that was brilliant."

C was skeptical. "What if a person at the agency went to school there and asks you a lot of question? You won't know anything."

She had a good point and Buckley stood there in the kitchen like a traffic cop had just whistled him to stop. The problem was her argument was going to run him over. So I pulled him to safety. "C...I *need* to find out." Our eyes locked again like we could read each others minds. She didn't say another word against the plan—even though I know she had doubts. She knew how much it meant.

I felt a swell of pride and obligation—the kind that I'm sure vets who have been in life and death combat situations must feel for their comrades.

The next day we had to get all our family video for our cover so we had Uncle Jimmy drop us off at Disney for the day. I had the portable camera my mom asked me to take pictures with and Buckley had to take video for his mom to watch when he got home. C had it easy. She only needed to pick up a couple souvenirs and some post cards. I have to admit Buckley is pretty smart. He had us each bring two other shirts to wear so in the video it wouldn't all look like the same day. We even went to the Epcot Center so it would look like we went to different parks for different days.

We did manage to have some fun on a few of the rides in-between our rigorous filming schedule. Space Mountain was freaky. You are on a rollercoaster in this dark building and you don't know when to expect it to turn and drop. And on the ten story chair drop I thought my insides were gonna come outside.

There were times when I actually felt like a kid on spring break having the time of my life. When we were screaming at the top of our lungs and laughing our heads off I almost forgot all the things that went wrong this year. And I almost forgot about finding out I was adopted.

On Monday we had Jimmy leave us at Disney. When the car disappeared we waved down a cab that was dropping some people off at the park.

"147 Martin Luther King Blvd., down town," Chondra told the cabby.

"Oh-key doe-key," said the little Indian man from the front seat.

When the cab pulled away from the run down building my nerves started to go into over time. Gazing up at the huge stone archway I looked up at the numbers. There was a 1 and a 4 but where the seven was supposed to be there was only a dark outline. I wanted to look in the bushes for the number so I could try and get him back where he belonged.

Buckley rummaged through his back pack and repeated a mental checklist to himself. "Clip board, check, video recorder, check, fake school badge, check."

C sat down on the crumbly steps. "What do we do while you're inside?"

"Just keep track of when people come and go. Write it down in the little note book." Then Buckley was swallowed by the old wooden double doors.

C and I walked across the street and down a little bit to a bus stop bench. Our vantage point was perfect to watch the door. I was glad that it was day time. Most of the people we saw would have been scary at night. They seemed barely human. The first guy we noticed had gray hair and was pushing a shopping cart that said "K-Mart." It had all kinds of old things inside that didn't look like he bought them at the store. He was talking to himself and kept answering in different voices. He looked at us and announced through his mostly missing teeth. "Beware! The end is coming!" He gazed up at the sky. "They'll be here soon." Then he started to argue with himself. "Stop telling them that you dummy. You'll scare them." In the dark I would have pictured three or four people walking the streets. Another guy that reminded me of the grim reaper in a black hoody was standing in the back of the little covered room where people wait for the bus. You could only see the lower half of his face which had a permanent scowl and a scar on the cheek. The front of his hoody was torn up the middle exposing his chain adorned chest. He reminded me of a black Houdini. I wondered if he was dropped in a tank of water if he could get out of all those chains.

I refocused my attention toward the front door.

After a while of sitting C leaned her shoulder against me. "Ben…What do you plan to do when you find out?"

I waited a minute to answer. I hadn't really thought much about that. My focus was on finding them. "I guess I want to ask them why?" I was watching the door but my mind was someplace else. "I don't want to leave my family. The Thompsons are all I have known…I just—."

"Need to know so you can put it to rest."

"Yes."

An hour later I came to one conclusion. There weren't many people being adopted. Only one person—an older heavy set women in a dress went into the building slightly after we sat down. We figured she probably worked there.

C fondled a piece of broken pavement between her fingers. "Buckley sure is taking a long time."

"You don't suppose he had some trouble do you?" I continued to watch her hand hold the piece of pavement like a baby bird that fell from the nest.

She continued to watch the door—unaware of the attention I was giving her hands. "No. I'm sure he's OK."

And like on cue he emerged from the building—he was a lost child on the steps of the adoption agency until we stood and waved to him.

We stayed outside together for a couple more hours. Homeless fixtures on the side of the street.

At twelve the only two ladies working left.

When they left they put up a little hand written sign on the door.

I watched them walk down the street. When they were out of sight I checked the sign on the door "Gone to lunch: be back in an our." *This is perfect* I thought. *If their security is as bad as their spelling this will be easy.*

I returned to Buckley and C. "They're gone. We just need to find a way inside."

Buckley was all teeth. He took out a role of black electrical tape and spun it on his finger like some kind of gun slinger.

Chondra had her hands on her hips. "Come on Buck. What's up?"

He motioned his head toward the door and we followed him. He turned the knob and pulled.

To C and my amazement it popped right open.

He had this "Taadaaa" look on his face.

"How did you—." I started to say.

He was pointing at the inside of the door frame like he was Vanna White showing us some letters to a puzzle.

The hole where the door lock was supposed to insert was covered with two pieces of electrical tape.

Buckley had the big cheesy grin back on his face. "Come inside."

C and I went into the office and followed him to the back area with lots of shelves and cabinets that said "Restricted." The only thing that made it any different than the rest of the dusty shabby office was the sign.

Buckley walked over to an ordinary faded gun metal Stealcase file cabinet. "Your answers are in here."

My heart was pounding in my ears. I couldn't believe we had done it. The name of my mother was inside this little cabinet. I quickly pulled on the handle. It was locked.

Buckley made his way to the disheveled desk in the middle of the room, and pulled it open. In the little tray inside the center drawer was a ring of small keys.

He was still grinning. But now he was humming that theme song to Mission Impossible again.

"The last time you started humming that song you know what happened." Chondra grabbed the keys from him. "Come on let's hurry." She brushed her hair back and began trying them. As luck would have it was the last one. When she turned it the lock jumped out. And we all jumped with it.

Buckley's grin was gone and the room was silent as I pulled open the squeaky top door. I looked at the first file. On the tab was a date. It was from a year after I was born. I skimmed the tabs. All of them were the same year. But the one in the back was from January.

I closed the top drawer and knelt down on the floor to open the bottom one. It squeaked just like the top one. I felt like one of those people that are called to the morgue to identify a body. The man lifts the white sheet and you say mournfully "Yeah…" and start to cry. "That's him." And you break down crying even harder as the medical examiner recovers the body. Only—I was trying to identify myself.

I gazed at the tab for the first file. It was from the year I was born.

My body began to show early signs of Parkinson disease as I fumbled through the files. When I came to September the disease had progressed to later stages and I was shaking uncontrollably. I put my hand on the file that said September 4. My birthday. I tried to pull it out but it wouldn't budge. It was like it didn't want to be found.

C put her hand on top of my functionless digits and helped me pull the file from the cabinet.

Inside was the name of my birth mom. All I had to do was open it. I took a deep breath and looked at C and Buck. Tears were welling in my eyes. I tried to keep my composure and wiped them with my sleeve but it didn't seem to matter. The tears just kept coming like somebody had left the faucet on.

C gave me a hug and Buck patted me on the shoulders like he was burping a hundred and twenty pound baby. "Thanks guys..." I was still blubbering. "This means the world to me."

I slowly regained my composure. "This is it." I grasped the folder edges and prepared to open it. "Do you want me to open it?"

"Go ahead Ben." C was wiping a couple of stray tears off her own cheeks.

I put my thumb on the tab to pull it open.

Then something else opened. It was the front door. And standing there was the office lady with a puzzled angry look on her face. "*What* are you doing—?" Before she could finish her sentence she was across the room and snatching the folder out of my hands. She sure moved fast for a big women. "I came back for my purse—it's a good thing." I felt like I was being scolded by my grandmother. "Who do you think you are? These are confidential records." She trained her eyes on Buckley. "You're in big trouble mister."

In a matter of seconds she was on the phone with the police. All the three of us did was stand there stunned. "That's right 147 Martin Luther King Blvd." She hung up the phone with authority. "Don't you even think of trying to run."

The thought had crossed all our minds until the other office lady showed up holding a to-go bag from Churches Chicken. "What the—who are these kids?"

The other lady answered. "Lock the door behind you Wilma."

Our heads sunk.

"These hoodlums were vandalizing the files."

"You don't say," replied the chicken lady.

I lifted my head trying to plead our case. "We're not *vandals!*" I stood with sound resolve.

There was a whimpering in my lips. "We…I…just want to find my birth mother…" My body and spirits sank in quicksands of emotional exhaustion.

The lady was scolding us but I didn't hear any of the words. She sounded like the teacher in Charlie Brown—maaaaaw waaaaaw waaaawt waaaaaw—.

I didn't hear a word until a banging at the door snapped me back to my senses. It was the police. This time there was no escape. Then I drifted back into myself. I watched as they cuffed us and took us in squad car. All I could do was think about how close I was to finding the answers. *Why didn't I just rip it open quickly and read the name? Why didn't I run and read the name before they caught me? Why? Why? Why?*

We sat in separate cells for several hours until they sorted out what we were doing. After questioning us separately and coming up with the same story they let us make some calls to our parents. My mom and dad were just glad that the Chicken Lady dropped the charges and that we were not hurt. They were so understanding it made me feel guilty about deceiving them.

Chondra's dad was the maddest. She said all he kept saying was, "I never should have let you go. You're to come home immediately. And I don't want you hanging out with those two any more." Her parents arranged for her flight to be changed and Jimmy took her to the airport that night. All she did was cry the whole way. I never thought anybody could cry that long.

Buckley got off easy. He said his mom started to give him the third degree but when she heard why we were arrested she got all quiet and told him everything was all right. She said he could stay with me the rest of the break—that I probably needed a friend.

Buck and I stayed the last three days of vacation. Mostly we just hung out by the pool or went down to the community rec. center to play ping pong. We figured Jimmy had orders to not let us get too far away.

During our ping pong games I went through this Zen transformation. Buck started calling me Buddha. I know it sounds ridiculous.

Buck would say things like. "We need to come up with a new plan. We were so close."

I'd answer in a far away voice. "Maybe it was meant to be. Maybe it was a sign that I wasn't meant to know. I think what I *need* is what I *have* not what I *think* I want.

He'd look at me in that scrunched up thinking hard way. "What are you talking about? I don't understand you."

"You have to find peace in what you are. Let's just enjoy the game."

This kind of talk would get him upset and he would walk off and do his own kind of obsessive meditation. "$E=mc^2$…"

Most of the time though we laughed about the unique experiences we had and how we were probably the only kids in the world who had been chased by officer Wimpley and apprehended by the Chicken Women.

Buck said it would make a brilliant story for a book. I told him "maybe someday I'll write it down."

# May-Day—My Day

May snuck around the corner and we often found ourselves basking in the sunlight in the courtyard at school during lunch. The Frisbees were flying and the hacksters were hacking. When you're in high school and the sun is shining you feel like its shinning just for you.

No one even paid attention to me anymore. Well, with the exception of Zonker. He still walked by, pointed, drooled, and said stuff like "hey Thompson, fall on your head lately?" and laughed to himself, "haha haha haha."

C would mock him when he did this by talking real slow back to him. "Goooood—one—Zonker. You're—so—clever."

Of course he didn't get that she was mocking him.

I didn't ever say anything to him. I was getting pretty good at ignoring. Besides all everyone else was talking about were McKayla and Rocket Arm. She dumped him for this college guy from Western. When we found out the guys name we hit the floor. His name is Ted Wimpley Jr.

After school I would go to C's and help her with math. She

136

helped me with writing. If we had any trouble with science we both went over to Buckley's. The problem was that things just weren't the same over there. Ever since we came back from spring break Mrs. Poindexter just seemed to stare out the window.

It made me sad to see her this way. One day C and I were over there playing around on Buckley's computer. He was trying to write a program for a new video game about these kids who are helping there friend find his parents. There are lots of levels where they have to escape from a fiendish football coach, barbarian barbers, unfriendly undertoads, sinister security guards, and a chicken lady. Honestly, I don't know where he gets all his ideas.

Buck was really getting into the graphics of the game and asked if I could go up and have his mom scrounge us up a snack.

I left him and C working on the computer.

Up stairs Mrs. P was at her usual place staring out the kitchen window. She kept washing the same glass over and over and over again. I looked at her pruny hands. "Uuuuuh…" I felt sort of helpless. "Buck sent me up for some snacks—Are you OK Mrs. Poindexter?"

She didn't look like Barbie any more. She had so much sadness in her eyes. I was starting to realize that people were pretty complex. They weren't like action figures or dolls that had only one permanent expression on their face.

She started to cry right into the soapy sink water.

I didn't know what to do. There was a time when I would have died to have her cry on my shoulder. Now I just saw someone in pain and I wanted to help. "It's OK Mrs. Poindexter…I know what it's like to hurt…When I found out I was adopted I was wrapped full of questions and anger."

She turned her head toward me. Her beautiful blue eyes were surrounded by red. Her blond hair dangled in the dishwater.

"Buckley and C helped me through that. They made me not feel so alone."

She grabbed the dish towel and wiped her eyes. "Why don't you have a seat while I get you kids a snack plate?"

I pulled up a chair at the kitchen table, as she started taking things out of the fridge. I looked out the window at Mr. Poindexter on the back of his riding mower making a checkerboard pattern in the grass. "You sure have a nice yard...It reminds me of a giant chess board."

She was cutting up some fruit for the plate. "Mr. Poindexter loves his yard. I think it gives his some quiet time from all the pressure of his job."

"Yeah, I'm not sure what I want to do yet...I guess I'm young enough that I don't have to decide right away."

She smiled a little as she opened the pantry to get some crackers for the yogurt dip she had in the middle of the platter. "You've got plenty of time to decide that. Most grown ups hardly know what they want to do. They keep changing their minds and second guessing themselves." She fanned out some Wheat Thins along the edge of the platter.

I turned my head and watched Mr. Poindexter finish his last sweep of the yard. "It's meant everything to me having Buckley help search for my mom. It's been like having a brother."

I heard the platter hit the tile floor and shatter. Shrapnel went in every direction like something blowing up from the inside.

I whirled my head toward the source of the explosion.

Mrs. Poindexter knelt down on the floor picking up the jagged jigsaw of pieces. "I've made such a mess of things." Tears were welling in her eyes again and made them all puffy. She kept repeating, "I've made such a mess."

138

I knelt down to help her. "It's OK Mrs. P. I've dropped lots of plates…" I tried to make her feel better. "You must know by now I've had my share of accidents."

She was inconsolable. "I've made such a mess…"

I handed her some large chucks of the platter.

She lifted her heavy head. "There's something that I want to tell you—."

A double set of steps came in the room. I turned to see who it was.

"What's all the noise?" Buck looked down at me and his mom.

"Woe" C knelt down on the floor next to me. "Let me help."

I turned back to Mrs. Poindexter. "What did you want to say?"

Buck and C looked at her.

It looked like she was shuffling around whatever she wanted to say in her head. "Out of all the places in the world I think it is incredible that we moved to this town and this street."

The kitchen slider opened and Mr. P was standing there looking down at the four of us. "Kind of a crazy place to have a picnic," he said with a puzzled look on his face.

Mrs. P stood up and tossed a hand full of pieces in the trash.

Mr. Poindexter noticed her swollen eyes and looked back down to the floor as we picked up the last of the chards. "Was that your grandmothers?" He asked. Then he turned his head toward Buckley with accusing eyes.

Mrs. P noticed his gaze. "I dropped it. I was making a snack for the kids and it slipped."

"Sorry about your plate Natalie. I know you don't have very many things of hers left." He patted her on the back as she rested her head on his shoulders.

C put her pieces in the trash. "Well—we better be goin?" She was trying to give them some space. "We'll see you later Mrs. P." She grabbed my shoulder and yanked me off the floor."

I had to pull away from her for a second to put the junk in my hands in the trash. Mrs. P had her eyes closed on her husbands shoulder. There was a tug on my shirt. C was nodding her head toward the door.

When we got outside C looked at me with her w*hat are you thinking?* look. I had a million questions in my head. *What did she mean by "I've made such a mess?" What was it that she wanted to tell me? Why was it so incredible that they moved to our street?*

"What is it Ben?" C's arm brushed against mine.

I told her what I was thinking as we made our way down by the river. We sat down on the make shift bench made of bent boards all of us had built at the end of the last summer. I felt the splintery wooden seat. "We made this the weekend we met Buckley." My fingers stopped and felt a crooked nail that was half pounded into its hole. "This one was going in straight then it must have been hit wrong and had to be pounded off to the side into a different place so it didn't stick out too far." I kept looking at the poor little nail that didn't get to go where it was supposed to. "Do you think that the nail was meant to be where it is?"

Chondra either knew more or just knew me because she had the right thing to say. "I don't think you can force them to go is some places. There are places that they just weren't meant to be. The wood's too twisted and knotted up that it wont take um." Her hand moved slowly across the bench and rested on top of mine. "I don't think any of us were born knowing how to do it perfect. I think that's something we have to learn as we go."

We were silent for a while—her hand on top of mine looking out at the river. After a while I turned toward her. Her long brown hair hung around her shoulders. I looked in her eyes and felt this strange pull—like I had felt once the first time I saw Mrs. Poindexter, but some how this was different. It wasn't the same way I had felt when I looked at McKayla. It wasn't the way I felt when I went out with Chrissie. It ran through every ounce of my being. It was like she could look inside of me and not mind what she saw.

The sun filtered through the freshly formed spring leaves and shined directly on her plump red lips. Her eyes met mine. I leaned toward her slightly and started to close my eyes as if by reflex. I fought them back open. I didn't want them closed. My lips closed in on hers. Her eyes stayed locked with me. I felt her hand squeeze on the top of mine. Our lips were so close we were breathing the same air. I wanted to kiss her more than anything in the world. Then she leaned away and smiled at me with this *what took you so long* look.

I smiled back. I was learning a lot this year. I wasn't getting things right the first time but like Thomas Edison said about all his inventions. "If you don't fail you don't learn what *not* to do." I guess I learned more than most this year.

I leaned back toward C for that kiss but she stood up, laughed with a sort of contented smile on her face, yanked me back to my feet, and ran down to our rope swing and swung into the river. I paused for a moment until she came up from under the current.

Marc had been right. Life this year had been like an animal trying to survive on the Savannah. *For now* I thought to myself *I just need to survive being me.*

C gave me a flirtatious wink from the water. "Are you coming in or what?"

I stood there, and for once I was glad I was me. I guess I still had a lot to learn. But I couldn't wait to get started.

9 781451 263121